PETER C[illegible] n 1942. He has [illegible] cher in history [illegible] rnalist, specialis[illegible] written thrillers, [illegible] stralia, quiz books, radio and television scripts, and the historical novels *The Gulliver Fortune*, *Naismith's Dominion*, *The Brothers Craft*, and *Wimmera Gold.* He is also the co-author of *Fred Hollows, An Autobiography.*

In 1999 Peter Corris was awarded the Ned Kelly Lifetime Achievement Award by the Crime Writers Association of Australia.

Salt and Blood is the twenty-fifth in his successful series of books about Sydney-based private eye Cliff Hardy.

'Cliff Hardy' series

The Dying Trade
White Meat
The Marvellous Boy
The Empty Beach
Heroin Annie
Make Me Rich
The Big Drop
Deal Me Out
The Greenwich Apartments
The January Zone
Man in the Shadows
O'Fear
Wet Graves
Aftershock
Beware of the Dog
Burn and Other Stories
Matrimonial Causes
Casino
The Washington Club
Forget Me If You Can
The Reward
The Black Prince
The Other Side of Sorrow
Lugarno

SALT AND BLOOD

A CLIFF HARDY NOVEL

Peter Corris

BANTAM BOOKS
SYDNEY • AUCKLAND • TORONTO • NEW YORK • LONDON

SALT AND BLOOD
A BANTAM BOOK

First published in Australia and New Zealand in 2002
by Bantam

National Library of Australia
Cataloguing-in-Publication Entry

Corris, Peter, 1942– .
Salt and Blood: a Cliff Hardy novel.

ISBN 1 86325 374 2.

1. Hardy, Cliff (Fictitious character) – Fiction.
2. Private investigators – New South Wales – Sydney – Fiction.
3. Alcoholics – Fiction. 4. Missing Persons – Fiction.
I. Title.

A823.3

Transworld Publishers,
a division of Random House Australia Pty Ltd
20 Alfred Street, Milsons Point, NSW 2061
http://www.randomhouse.com.au

Random House New Zealand Limited
18 Poland Road, Glenfield, Auckland

Transworld Publishers,
a division of The Random House Group Ltd
61–63 Uxbridge Road, Ealing, London W5 5SA

Random House Inc
1540 Broadway, New York, New York 10036

Edited by Carl Harrison-Ford
Cover design by Cusp Creative Pty Ltd
Cover photograph by Robert Pearce/*Sydney Morning Herald*
Text designed and typeset in Garamond 11 on 13 by Midland Typesetters, Maryborough, Victoria
Printed and bound by Griffin Press, Netley, South Australia

10 9 8 7 6 5 4 3 2 1

For James Hall, once again, who helped to get it all started.

Thanks to Michael Dilli for information about surfing, to Michael Brown for help with geography and to Jenny Coopes who made a comment about Elvis she may not recall. Thanks also to Jean Bedford and Carl Harrison-Ford.

PART 1

1

I met Glen Withers in a Paddington pub near the Victoria Barracks after she'd been to her second AA meeting for the week. She runs her own private enquiry agency in the eastern suburbs. We were lovers, never were enemies; now we're friends.

'How was it?' I asked.

'Loads of fun. Michael told us all about his recipe for making battery acid drinkable.'

'I hope you scribbled it down. What'll you have?'

'Soda and bitters, no lime.'

It was Thursday night and busy. I'd grabbed a table in the partitioned-off, no-smoking area, but I had to go into the battle zone to get the drinks. Scotch and ice for me. Two at the most. Glen could walk home from here but I wouldn't be going with her and I'd have to drive back to Glebe. It was after nine o'clock and the noise level was going up the way it does as the alcohol level rises. The crowd was youngish and mixed — men and women and a few indeterminates, gays and straights. Here and there I spotted a face old enough to remember Bob Menzies and six o'clock closing. Not many; some wouldn't even remember Bob Hawke.

I pushed my way back to the table, keeping the drinks clear of shoulders and elbows and waving hands. Glen always insisted on our meetings taking place in full-on drinking situations, to keep her on her toes. We touched glasses.

'Thanks, Cliff,' she said. 'Still like that stuff, do you?'

I examined the contents of my glass. 'I'm glad it exists,' I said.

'Mr Enigmatic.'

'That's me. How're you doing? D'you miss it?'

'Less and less. It's nice to have the time and space for other things. I didn't for a while.'

We sipped our drinks and let the noise wash around us. Danger time. We'd get to feeling comfortable together. Close even. Consider the possibilities. Weigh up those feelings against the loneliness. I took a solid slug and broke the mood.

'So,' I said. 'Here you are looking ten years younger in your sobriety and as I'm ten years older than you that puts twenty years between us. What can I do for you, Glen?'

'Stop being a clown for a start.'

Good punch, I thought. *That gives her the points she needs.* 'What's this about?'

It was a familiar pattern. We lurched between affection and hostility and found ways to get along well professionally and adequately otherwise. We put work each other's way and what with the GST and the intrusion of big international agencies into the field, the pie was shrinking for the smaller players. Glen smiled; a fine network of lines fanned out from her eyes and deep grooves appeared in her cheeks. Her fair hair, cut short, had silver streaks; she wore a black silk shirt, jeans and a grey leather jacket, no jewellery. If you were scouting for women perhaps you wouldn't notice her right off, but if you did look you'd look again.

'I've got a client,' she said. 'Or rather I'm trying to land one.'

'I know the feeling. "I just want your advice, Mr Hardy. I'm not sure that I actually *need* a private detective but . . ." Trying for free service.'

Glen shook her head. The fair hair bounced and I wanted to stroke it, smell it. 'No,' she said. 'It's not like that. Money's not a problem.'

'I love that phrase — "money's not a problem". It's just that my lips have difficulty forming the sounds.'

'I told you to stop clowning.'

Her telling me to do things had broken us up in the first place. Water under the bridge. I nodded and finished my drink. One to go.

'This guy came to see me. Warren Harkness, a lawyer. I rate pretty well with lawyers these days, Cliff. Better than you, I bet. They think they can keep the lady investigator under control, which is what they want. Naturally. Warren's got a brother named Rodney who's due to be released from a mental institution. A private facility. Rutherford House. Ever heard of it?'

'No.'

'Up Bilgola Way. Very exclusive and expensive.'

'Money's no object.'

'Right.'

'The Harkness family got Rodney . . . installed there seven years ago. He cracked up after his wife left him, taking their kid. He got on the grog, went through a lot of money, did some damage to the family business, became psychotic, so they . . .'

'Who's they?'

'Right. Ah . . . his mother and this brother — Lady Rachel Harkness and Mr Warren, middle name St John.' She pronounced it *Sinjin.*

I didn't. 'St John?'

'Don't start with your anti-establishment rap. Okay, they're very rich. Property.'

'That's the best kind of rich I always think. Harder to steal. And what's your involvement and where do I come in?'

'Get yourself another drink and I'll tell you. Your tongue's hanging out.'

'That's just in expectation of hearing you saying Sinjin like that again.'

Glen had only drunk half of what was in her glass so it was just another Scotch for me. Cheap date. I made it a double. There's something about people going to AA meetings that makes me drink more. When I got back to the table Glen had her notebook out and was flicking over the pages. Her fingers were long with closely trimmed nails. No rings. She glanced up and saw me looking.

'What?'

'You've got nice hands.'

'Good line but I don't put them around men's

dicks any more. I'll shake with you when we finish if you like. This is how it is — the Harknesses want me to try to find Rodney Harkness's wife and kid. They've got ideas of reuniting them.'

'What does Rodney think about that?'

'He doesn't know about it. He doesn't get out for a couple of days.'

'Cured, is he?'

Glen shrugged. 'They hope so but they're not sure. They're not the ones behind getting him out. Apparently some civil liberties lawyers got involved. Took his case on as a natural justice issue and filed papers and got reports and a court order. The Harknesses want me to find out about that as well.'

'Here's to civil liberties and two jobs,' I toasted her. 'Nice going.'

'Three,' Glen said. 'They also want someone to keep an eye on Rodney for a while to make sure he doesn't start drinking, or to help if he goes nuts again. I thought you might take it on.'

'Do you get the other jobs if I don't?'

'I don't get them unless I provide someone for the minding job. I don't want just anyone, I want you.'

That was Glen. She had a way of getting me on the back foot. After all the rows we'd had I was always looking for an edge with her, like trying to get her to admit she needed me now. And she usually outmanoeuvred me just like this.

We talked it over for a while but I knew I was going to agree. I had nothing else substantial on hand and this could be a few weeks of steady work at my standard rates, subcontracted by Glen.

It beat process serving and escorting suits to meetings with other suits and I'd always wanted to meet someone with St John in their name.

'Tell me Rodney's a St John, too.'

'I don't know. You'll have to find out. Are you in?'

I said I was interested and Glen said she'd get the paperwork to me tomorrow. In an effort to stay in the race, I'd recently invested a decent cheque in home and office PCs and signed up for the web and email but this was just about the first occasion to use it properly.

We said our goodbyes with kisses on the cheeks outside the pub with the bright young things still sparking inside. I watched her walk away in her designer jeans, low heels and sporty leather jacket and felt a chill through my body although it was September and a mild enough night, with slightly chilly wind gusts. I wanted to run after her and say, Fuck all this. Let's sell up and go to the Central Coast and open an agency together and make enough to live on and catch fish and stay brown all the year round. I took one step or maybe I just thought I did. Then she was out of sight and I was turning around as if in response to her disappearance and I could see the faded blue of my Falcon parked a hundred metres away.

By the time I'd reached the car, reality and the cold breeze had cut in, dissolving the nostalgia and the sentimentality and diluting the alcohol. I started the car and let it warm up and I was already thinking about the problems of dealing with someone who'd been shut away for seven years.

Home alone. It wasn't late and I wasn't sleepy. I took a walk around the block to induce sleep. The last three hundred metres of Glebe Point Road on the right-hand side going down to the water are undergoing massive development. An up-market apartment complex is replacing the warehouses and boat yards. A working area of the bay has had its time and the water is more valuable now as something to look at. The painting-by-numbers advertisement for the complex stresses the view as the selling point. The developers promise walkways and grass plus a fountain and it'll probably look okay, but I'll miss the boat yards. If I sold my terrace I could probably buy two apartments — live in one, rent the other and be set for life, except that it'd feel like death.

Back inside, I only looked briefly at the Scotch bottle before making a pot of coffee. I went upstairs to the spare bedroom where I'd set up the computer and turned it on. I heard the coffee perking and went down to fill a mug. I'm told there are people who can sit down at a computer without anything to eat, drink or smoke but I'm not one of them.

A bit of a trawl turned up some Harkness data. Warren St J was a partner in Beams, Harkness and Trezize, solicitors in the city. Nice web site. Not exactly touting for custom but letting the world know they were around. Harkness Holdings Ltd was a publicly listed company with interests in commercial and residential property in Sydney and Melbourne and with a solid share value. Sceptic that I am, I wondered immediately why such a well-heeled character would deal with a one-woman detective agency. Why not one of the internationals with their Dick Tracy wrist walkie-talkies and lapel badge cameras? I sipped coffee and thought about it. Three possibilities: one — referral. Maybe Glen had done good work for someone Harkness knew. Two — security. The bigger the show the more people in the know. Three — containment. In my experience clients sometimes went for a small outfit so they could feel in control.

I wondered whether Glen had got herself a web site yet. Sure enough: The Glen Withers Agency — former Detective Inspector NSW Police; BSc (Newcastle), BJuris (Monash); Captain, Army Reserve. Confidential enquiries discreetly conducted, blah, blah. Nice photo. I stared at the screen and tried to imagine my own home page: Hardy Investigations — Second Lieutenant Australian Army (campaign ribbon, mentioned in despatches); LLB (NSW) discontinued; twenty-plus years experience. I saw my battered, broken-nosed phiz cold-eyeing back at me and shook my head. Bad move.

I finished my coffee and was about to log off when an idea occurred to me. I called up the search engine and tapped in Rutherford House. There was a fair amount of Rutherford this and Rutherford that but I got to it before too long. It was amazing how such a glossy, up-market, hi-tech website could convey so little warmth. The grounds and buildings looked nice and the medical staff had every qualification under the sun. The place had government certification and high profile patrons and endorsements but something about the design and layout of the information struck me as chilling. I had no doubt it cost a fortune to be treated there, but for all the pictures of garden beds and recreation areas it still gave off the atmosphere of a prison. I printed out the page with the staff list and bookmarked the site.

Before switching off I checked the email, not expecting anything. There was a message with an attachment from withersg. The contract, no doubt. She'd probably drawn it up beforehand. Sure of her man. The message read 'Thanks, Cliff.' There we were, in the inner west and the eastern suburbs, connected by computer but far, far apart.

2

In the morning I printed out the contract and read it through. I'd get my retainer from her and she'd meet my ongoing daily rate and expenses. The document contained no details of the case so I was signing on simply on the strength of what Glen had told me. Glen and I had worked in tandem like this a few times before, sometimes with her as the principal and sometimes me, without any trouble. But those times we'd only signed a contract halfway through the job or at the end or not at all. I wasn't happy about signing such an open-ended contract up front. All this high-tech formality. I brooded about it and Glen rang me as I was brooding.

'I thought you could sign it and fax me back.'

'I'm sorry. I reckon I should know a bit more about it before committing myself.'

I could feel her impatience coming down the line but she composed herself, obviously with an effort. 'Tell you what, I'm scheduled to meet Lady R and her son this afternoon at the family home,' she said. 'I'd like you to come along so they can see how reliable you look. And you can look them over and decide.'

'Okay, I'll brush up on reliability. Where and when?'

When turned out to be 3 p.m. and where was a large house with a Mediterranean villa look to it set in what appeared from the street to be half an acre of forest in the middle of Bellevue Hill. I drew up in the Falcon behind Glen's Pajero. A high brick fence enclosed the grounds and the only entrance was a narrow walk-through gate with heavy security. No driveway. I got out of my car and leaned in at the Pajero's driver window.

'Where's the entrance to the underground car park?'

'I was told about that. They don't have cars. There's a delivery entrance off the side street that runs along the east boundary of the place. Weird, huh?'

'You mean Warren lives here with his mum?'

'That's right.'

'Where's dad?'

Glen busied herself collecting her shoulder bag and checking in it for her professional bits and pieces. 'I imagine we're going to find out about him and Rodney and other stuff. All I know is he's dead. Let's have a look at you. Are you presentable?'

I stepped back and she got out and looked me over. A navy blazer, blue shirt, dark slacks and shoes, no tie. I'd shaved closely and washed my hair which was still more dark than grey. Glen was wearing a black pants suit, low heels, white silk blouse.

'You'll do,' she said. 'Let's go in.'

'This is where you say, "I'll do the talking."'

'You'll say what you like when you choose. You always do.'

The gate had an ivy-covered wrought-iron and timber canopy with an electronic buzzer set in the brickwork. Glen hit the buzzer and said her name into the intercom. The gate swung open. We walked up sixty or seventy metres of paving that had just the right amount of moss growing between the slate blocks, with closely weeded garden beds and lawn like putting greens on either side, to a set of ten sandstone steps worn concave by well-shod feet. A wide, tiled verandah ran the length of the house and before you could enter you had to negotiate a heavy security screen and yet another buzzer.

Press and wait. After a minute or more the door opened, giving me time to look around and see the surveillance camera mounted a metre above our heads. The Harknesses clearly didn't like surprise visitors or maybe they didn't like visitors at all. The woman who opened the door didn't exactly wear a maid's uniform but she didn't look quite like a civilian either. Severe belted dress in a dark fabric, cream scarf, dark stockings, sensible shoes. She was neither young nor old, fat nor thin, as if she'd been designed to blend into the background.

'Ms Withers and . . .?'

'Mr Hardy,' Glen said.

She nodded. 'Lady Rachel and Mr Harkness are in the east sitting room. Will you come this way, please.'

We stepped out of the twenty-first century into the nineteenth. The entrance hall was vast and cold with a wide staircase ascending into shadows on one side and a dimly lit passage on the other. The parquet floor made Glen and the woman's leather heels ring and my rubber ones squeak. We followed our guide about the length of a cricket pitch to a wood panelled door where she knocked discreetly before opening it. Up to this point the place had been cold, lacked light and smelled of money and floor polish, but this room carried an aroma of coffee and tobacco and the afternoon light flooded in from French windows letting out to the verandah with the garden not far off.

We walked across an ornately worked carpet towards leather chairs and a couch where a man and a woman were sitting beside a trolley carrying a silver coffee pot and matching jugs, a sugar bowl likewise. Porcelain cups. The man was drinking coffee and smoking a chunky cigar, the woman was just sitting. The man put his cup down on the trolley and came forward holding his cigar in front of him like a torch. He was big, 190 centimetres or so, giving him a couple on me, and he could have spotted me a few kilos as well. Put him at ninety plus. A lot of it was soft though, discreetly masked by the pinstriped double-breaster.

'Ms Withers,' he said. 'Thank you for coming.'

Glen introduced me to Harkness and he introduced us both to his mother. At a guess, Lady Rachel Harkness was in her sixties, fashionably thin with the lacquered look rich women acquire from dieting, makeup and perhaps a little discreet plastic surgery. Her hair was a subtle blend of silver and blonde and everything about her — the silk dress, minimal jewellery, elegant pose and restrained expression — conspired to say, Look at me with envy. I am beautiful and rich.

The rapport between the two appeared to be very good although I had a suspicion they had rehearsed this meeting. Glen and I sat down and Warren Harkness served us coffee. I refused a cigar. With his mother saying almost nothing but making little confirmatory gestures with her head and hands, Harkness outlined the assignment.

'My brother married Lucille Hammond on the rebound as they say, from the collapse of another relationship. They weren't at all suited. Rodney was . . . is, a quiet, serious sort of chap, when he's ah . . . in control of himself. Lucille was wild, younger than him of course. Extroverted. She was Catholic and wouldn't use birth control. They had a child quite quickly, a girl. Rodney was delighted but Lucille didn't accept the responsibility. She chafed under it, you might say. They fought. I'm sorry to say that she provoked Rodney into hitting her. She left him. Rodney had some letters from her and he sent her some money. He was desperate to make amends. But she told him she never wanted to see him again and she broke off all contact. That's when Rodney began to drink and behave . . . erratically.'

Harkness paused to offer us more coffee and make sure his mother had everything she wanted. Nice manners, or perhaps a good sense of dramatic timing. I was irritated and I could feel Glen's similar reaction. We obviously weren't intended to interrupt the flow but Glen did anyway.

'Do you have these letters, Mr Harkness?' she asked. 'And the details of the money and so on?'

'Yes, yes, of course.' Harkness killed his cigar in a crystal ashtray and his mother wrinkled her nose at the smell — the first spontaneous movement she'd made. Control was her middle name.

'This is difficult for us,' Harkness went on. 'Rodney embezzled some money. He lost it gambling and tried to recoup it by dealing in drugs. The police became aware of it. There were various unpleasant incidents. Someone attempted to blackmail Rodney and he injured the person very severely. He attempted to bribe a police officer and then assaulted him. If matters had run their course he would have been sentenced to a prison term and no doubt have deteriorated further.'

Harkness was looking at me by this stage. I nodded but I thought, *I doubt he'd have served seven years.* I still wasn't being invited to comment but I did. 'You were able to make other arrangements.'

Harkness glanced at his mother who nodded slightly and spoke in her slightly stagy top-drawer accent. 'Yes. Several psychiatrists examined Rodney and he was declared unfit to plead to the charges. His responsibility was judged to be diminished. He was placed in institutional care and his state of mind was reviewed from time to time.'

The formal tableau was getting me down. I deliberately made my cup and saucer rattle as I put them back on the trolley. 'How's he doing?'

Harkness shook his head and some loose flesh moved on his face. Jowls on the way. 'Opinions differ. Our . . . some doctors say he is still delusional. Others decided otherwise.'

Lady Rachel Harkness's sculptured lips formed into a tight line. 'There has been interference from some quarter and we want Ms Withers to find out all she can about that. There may be professional misconduct involved.'

You want to lock the poor fucker up again, I thought, but Glen cut in smoothly.

'I'm sure there will be avenues to follow on that,' she said. 'And I understand you want to reunite Mr Harkness with his wife and child.'

'No,' Lady Rachel said sharply.

Warren looked uncomfortable and as if he'd like to get another cigar going, but perhaps one was all Mum allowed him. 'I may have given you a false impression there in our preliminary talk, Ms Withers,' he said. 'We are only interested in the child. We believe that Rodney might respond positively to meeting his daughter again.'

'And the mother?' I said.

'We'll cross that bridge when we come to it,' Lady Rachel said. 'All we want to say about her is that she was a most unsuitable person. No character, no background. Most unsuitable.' I'd swear her accent slipped a notch or two.

They went on to outline what they hoped I could do for them. Their biggest worry was that Rodney Harkness would get back on the grog despite his long drying-out. They had managed to modify the court release order the civil liberties people had secured to provide that, in addition to psychological counselling and monitoring, he should be assigned a companion for at least the first few weeks to keep him on the straight and narrow.

'How does he feel about that?' I asked.

'I understand he's reluctant but will comply.'

You understand, I thought. 'Have you seen him, Mr Harkness?'

'Briefly. He has refused to live here with us so I've rented him a flat in Bondi. He used to be a keen surfer. I'm hoping that can be part of his rehabilitation.'

I avoided looking at Glen. 'If he wants to drink there's no way to stop him.'

'He doesn't want to,' Lady Rachel said sharply. 'Your job will be to help him be strong. To stick to that resolution.'

I thought about it, feeling sceptical but maybe looking reliable. I had the feeling that I'd passed muster with the Harknesses and I could see relief pass over Glen's face and the mother and son exchanged nods. I don't like to be nodded over and I barely listened to what followed. I occupied myself by looking around the room, which was all in good taste but with nothing personal to it. I caught an angry look from Glen and swung my attention back to Harkness. I was to collect Rodney at Rutherford House on Sunday afternoon. Harkness would courier all the relevant documents along with photographs of Lucille née Hammond and the daughter, whose name was Rose, to Glen that evening. And that was about it.

Lady Rachel said something complimentary about Glen's reputation and her son nodded. They were big on nodding. I shook Harkness's doughy hand and touched his mother's cold fingers. We said our goodbyes; Harkness escorted us to the door and the woman in black took us out with more leather tapping on wood and rubber squeaking.

We'd been in there for almost an hour and the sun was getting lower in the sky, casting tall tree shadows across the lawn. The day had been warm but a cool breeze had got up. Rodney was going to need his wetsuit.

We walked down the path in silence until we got to the gate. 'You didn't exactly go out of your way to be charming,' Glen said.

I turned around and looked back at the house. There was something faintly ridiculous about a place that size being occupied by just two people. Or maybe something sinister.

'It's hard to be charming when a couple of shits are treating you like shit,' I said.

3

The cool air got chillier as Glen marched ahead to her car. I had to lengthen and quicken my stride to catch up with her.

'What?'

She dug in her bag for her keys and I saw that her hand was trembling when she pulled them out.

'Glen, I . . .' I reached to touch her but she pulled back.

'We have to talk.'

It was a dreaded phrase, one that had been spoken before all our fights. 'What about?' I said. 'This job is bullshit, Glen. You know what they're about. We . . .'

'That's what we have to talk about. Let's go to Bondi. The Gelato Bar. Okay?'

I shrugged. 'Sure.'

On the drive to Bondi I reviewed my impressions of Glen's clients. One of my failings, reinforced by being in this job for so long, is a habit of thinking the worst of people. I struggle against it and try to find the positive side, but I was having difficulty with the Harknesses. She seemed to be a patrician clothes horse. Cold and narcissistic. He was a soft mother's boy who looked to have had a very easy ride and their concern about the son and brother certainly had nothing to do with affection for him.

The more I thought about it the more I reckoned I should try to dissuade Glen from taking on the case. Another negative thought — I didn't think she should be a party to letting that pair get the grand-daughter/niece into their clutches. I was cruising Campbell Parade looking for a parking spot before a positive note of any kind entered my thinking — from what I'd heard I had a certain amount of sympathy for Rodney Harkness.

The Gelato Bar has been there ever since I can remember, and without much change of decor or style. If it ain't broke . . . I was a little surprised Glen hadn't suggested a resolution-confirming pub. It was late enough in the day for me. She was in a booth when I got there and had already fended off a few people who'd contested her right to occupy it as a single.

'I'm buying,' she said. 'What'll you have?'

'Long black.'

The waitress had been hovering and took the order quickly. Flat white for Glen. She began using the wrapped sugar cubes as building blocks. I reached over and dismantled the structure, putting the cubes back in the bowl.

'What's this about, Glen? What's the matter?'

She lifted her face and the stress showing in it aged her a couple of years. 'Let's wait till the coffee comes.'

We sat there with a silence building between us that I found impossible to interpret except that there was something serious behind it. The coffee came and Glen grabbed hers, stirred a couple of cubes of sugar into it and gulped at it. She drank half of the cup quickly before wiping her mouth on a napkin. 'I'm not doing too well with the alcohol thing,' she said.

'Oh, shit. I'm sorry. What about the ten steps and all that?'

'It helps but it's still fucking hard. I thought it'd get easier but it doesn't.'

I drank some coffee with the unhelpful thought that I wished it was whisky and didn't say anything. Glen finished her drink and started fiddling with the spoon in the froth. I didn't try to stop her. 'At first I was doing great. It was terrific not to be thinking about booze all the time. Not to be worried about being more than an hour away from a possible drink. I liked losing the weight, getting back into skirts I hadn't worn, hadn't been able to wear for a couple of years. I'm vain enough to be pleased that I looked better, especially after the break-up with Colin . . . You know.'

Glen had married a policeman after our affair finished. 'It's rough.'

'Mm. But gradually I started to take those things for granted and you know what I began to think?'

'I can guess,' I said. 'You started to think you could have all those plusses and maybe have a drink or two as well.'

'Yes!' she said fiercely. 'I haven't, I know that's

bullshit from the other times I stopped and started, but Christ it's so hard sometimes.'

'I know a bit about it,' I said.

'Yes, I know you do, but you seem to be able to stay in control. I was getting up to a bottle of gin a day, or more. A few times I woke up at home and couldn't remember anything much past noon.'

I hadn't heard about her alcoholism in this kind of detail before but I knew the pattern and how destructive it was and how hard to break. The waitress took Glen's cup and she clenched her fists. I ordered two more coffees although I was only halfway through mine. I drained it and passed a couple of sugar cubes across for her to play with.

She forced a smile. 'Thanks. The AA meetings helped tremendously at first, but I can't take all that higher power crap and there seems to be more of it creeping in. And I'm getting bored earlier and more easily. I'm having trouble sleeping.'

She took off the sunglasses she'd been wearing and her eyes looked tired and strained. I noticed that her makeup was heavier than usual. Last night in the flattering light of the pub and with a few drinks on board I'd thought she looked fine; here under the fluorescent light, cracks were showing.

I tried to say something comforting but she was in full flight.

'It's really horrible, Cliff. You wander around in your spare time trying to fill up the spaces. I fiddle with things that don't need doing just to be doing something, anything, to keep my mind off it. Talk about doing it a day at a time. Sometimes an hour feels like a fucking day, and a day feels like . . .'

She broke off as the coffees arrived. She dipped her head so the waitress couldn't see the pain in her face. We got to work with the sugar and spoons. I expected her to go on but she'd run out of steam.

'Are you seeing anyone about it, like a psychologist?'

'I've seen a couple, including a hypnotist. It doesn't do any good. I don't care *why* I'm an alcoholic, whether it's because I'm a repressed bisexual or have low self-esteem or whatever.'

'They say it's a disease. Could be genetic or . . .'

'Bullshit. It's a compulsion, an obsession. You give in to it or you fight it, but the fight's so hard. I'm sorry.'

'About what?'

'Dragging you here to lay all this on you. The point is I haven't been doing well with the agency lately. I've mucked a couple of things up because of this. Lost concentration. Cliff, the only way I can get through this is to work! When I'm busy it's not nearly so bad. So I need this job, I need it badly. It's ideal — lots of time-consuming digging and searching. Lots of possibilities and maybe some travel. Something to fill up those fucking empty holes. So I'm asking you to come in on it with me. There's no one else I can talk to like this. No one else to understand.'

I took the contract from my blazer pocket, unfolded it and signed. Glen grabbed a napkin and dabbed at her eyes.

'Thank you.'

'Right,' I said, 'but when you say come in on it

with you, I think you should mean that. You've got to keep me informed as you find things out and I'll do the same. And let me help if I can.'

'I will.' She signed below my signature. 'I'll fax you a copy for your files. If there's stuff you should see in the material I'm getting tonight I'll get it to you.'

'But they're still shits.'

She smiled and some of the tension slipped away. 'They are, aren't they? Did you notice how her accent slipped when she got angry?'

'Yep. They're hoping he can be shunted straight back inside. By the way, what did Rodney do before he got put away?'

'He was an actor — a bit of theatre, TV, commercials.'

'They must've loved that. I bet there's something about the family money involved here. Tell you now I won't come at that if I've got any say, not unless he's really off the rails.'

We finished the coffee and Glen put the contract in her bag, patted at her hair and put her sunglasses back although she wouldn't need them outside now. I stood and stretched discreetly the way I have to after sitting down for a spell these days. 'You can call me any time if you need to talk or want company.'

'Still on your own?'

'Mostly.'

I caught a glimpse of us in a mirror as we left the place. We looked like a couple but everyone knows mirrors lie.

I drove to the office and, now that I was committed to the Harkness job, I tidied up a few loose ends and replied to two faxes and an email, refusing offered jobs with regrets. Then I went to the gym for a late workout because I wasn't sure when I'd next get the chance. A quick one in the Toxteth and then it was home to cook, eat, read a few chapters of David Hickie's book about Chow Hayes, the gunman. Hayes had done his dash by the time I was rubbing shoulders with those types in Sydney and I wasn't sorry. A hard man. The book held my interest but I kept breaking off, half expecting a call from Glen. She didn't ring and I decided that it was a good sign — she'd found the strength to get through another night. I hoped I was right.

In the morning a courier brought a package containing a photograph, a set of keys and a credit card. The keys were labelled with the address of a flat in Bondi. *Christ*, I thought, *they're not even going to show him the place.* The photograph showed a dark-haired man and a fair-haired woman with a child of, to me, uncertain age. Just toddling perhaps. The man was thin and handsome in a Tony Perkins sort of way. The woman was willowy with an angry look to her. I hoped Glen had a better and later photograph of the daughter because it was impossible to even guess from this one what she might look like seven years later. The slip containing the PIN was enclosed with the card and I wondered how much money they'd put at Rodney's disposal. Easy enough to find out.

With the day to kill I paid two visits, one to my doctor in Glebe, Ian Sangster, and one to Frank Parker, an old friend who retired as a Deputy Commissioner of Police. I asked Ian, who'd dealt with quite a few mentally damaged people in his time, some of them well-heeled, if he knew anything about Rutherford House. He didn't. Said he'd ask.

Frank and Hilde Parker live in Tamarama, giving me a chance to kill two birds with one stone. On the way to their place I called in at the flat in a street off Curlewis Street, Bondi, a few blocks back from the beach, to see what his loving family had assigned to Rodney. Pretty nice — adequately furnished, two bedrooms, well fitted out kitchen and living room, decent balcony. A big Malibu surfboard took up space in one of the bedrooms and if Rodney wanted to go surfing he didn't have far to trot. Likewise if he wanted to go drinking. There was an envelope taped to the board and I took a look at it. A receipt from a city surfshop carrying the brand of the board, the name of the shaper and the identification number. No note saying, 'Love, Mum.'

Frank was swimming laps in his pool when I arrived. He climbed out, looking glad to stop. He told me that Hilde was off playing tennis. I asked about their son, Peter, whose anti-godfather I am.

'Backpacking,' Frank said.

'Where?'

'Europe.'

'You'd have given him a telecard so he can call home like Peter Reith did for his kid.'

Frank rubbed his hair dry. 'He reverses the charges when he bothers to call. Fancy a beer?'

We had a drink in the shade by the pool and I asked Frank if he knew anything about a case involving Rodney Harkness and assault on a police officer.

'Vaguely. Tell me more.'

I filled in what I knew and Frank nodded several time as he worked on his can. When I finished he gave me one of the wintry, enigmatic smiles that used to make offenders very uncomfortable. 'The name was familiar, especially the St John bit, and a little of what you're saying comes back to me. I can't add much to that. What I do remember is about the father, Ralph Harkness, Sir Ralph.'

'What about him?'

'Suicide,' Frank said. 'Very suss.'

4

Frank said he'd forgotten the details of Sir Ralph St John Harkness's death but had an impression that it had been well and truly hushed up. He said he'd check with some people who'd know. I gave him the number of the Bondi flat. On the way home I stopped at an ATM and checked on Rodney's credit rating. They'd deposited $7328 for him. It seemed a strange amount and I concluded that it might have been his money to start with, plus interest. Not much of a nest egg to face life with after seven years' incarceration. I wondered what other support the family intended to provide. At a guess, not much.

I phoned Glen when I got home but got her answering machine. I didn't leave a message but I sent her an email detailing what Frank had told me and about the flat and the bank account. I was keeping to my part of the bargain about sharing information and I hoped she'd keep to hers. In the evening, after Chow Hayes had shot a few more people, I settled down with my notebook and drew my usual diagram. It showed the names of the parties in the case so far arranged around the edges of the page, and dotted lines with arrows joining them up indicating their relationships, together with what snippets of information I had about them. I don't know that these jottings ever helped me work something out but they help me to remember things and they do provoke questions. In this instance a couple jumped out. Warren and Rodney Harkness were the only children of Sir Ralph and Lady Rachel, but did Warren have any offspring? Living with his mum like that it seemed unlikely, so wouldn't Rodney's daughter be the logical heir to the Harkness millions? If not, how come? And if so, why stay out of touch with her for seven years?

I didn't know much about wills and inheritance except that they were a frequent cause of family friction. My understanding was that you couldn't cut a blood relation out of your will without good cause and such an action could be readily challenged in the courts. I wondered if Lucille Hammond had divorced Rodney and made a note to find out. Even if she had, and wanted nothing to do with the Harknesses, wouldn't she still have an eye to her daughter's inheritance?

I had an impulse to send Glen another email about these questions but I suppressed it. She'd most likely have thought of them herself and if she hadn't she'd probably resent my interference. But it chafed at me and reminded me why I preferred to work alone — two heads might be better than one, but they can't instantly swap what's inside them.

As I mulled things over I thought how little of

people's lives show on the surface. I remember the people in our street in Maroubra and how my mother used to gossip about them while smoking her endless Craven A filters and sipping her Penfolds sweet sherries. Fred Harrison two doors away was sleeping with his wife's sister with the wife's knowledge and consent; Dulcie Lamb, the Salvation Army sergeant across the street, was an ex-prostitute; Sammy Porter on the corner, aspiring Eastern Suburbs footballer, wore his fat sister's clothes to parties, and so on. My father, who preferred to take people at their face value, claimed that she made a lot of it up, but these days I'm inclined to think that she was right on the money.

Driving north to Bilgola on a Sunday isn't as much fun as it should be or as it once was. Crazy laws back then. In the seventies we used to drive to Newport and register as bona fide travellers in order to drink. My ex-wife Cyn and I used to make the trip quite often. We'd meet up with friends in the beer garden of the pub. Cyn would get tanked on three gins and tonic and I'd drink far too much full-strength beer, there being no other kind, and drive home with a blood alcohol reading that would earn you a lifetime suspension today. The cops turned a blind eye quite literally, with a good number of them being pissed on duty themselves in those far-off days.

The problem now is the number of people who live and have business the length of the northern beaches. The road was clogged most of the way and many of the drivers apparently only got behind the wheel at the weekend. Their skills were minimal and their patience short. The day was warm, getting towards hot. The Falcon has no air-conditioning and with the window down I was taking a dozen different carcinogens into my lungs with every kilometre. A man might as well smoke. I'd recently had the cassette player fixed by possibly the last man in Sydney who knew how to do it, and I played an old Ry Cooder tape in which he sang about seeing famous people. Maybe I could do the same up on the northern beaches — run a bit further up to Palm Beach, get a glimpse of Rachel Ward or Bob Ellis; preferably Rachel.

The real Rutherford House resembled the place depicted on the website but not that closely. The photograph had been taken from the most flattering angle in a golden light. Up close it appeared much smaller and rather faded. The grounds could have done with a decent clean-up — some mowing, pruning and weeding — and the gravel on the drive had worn thin in spots, revealing cracked clay beneath. I tried to remember whether the website had boasted views of Pittwater. I thought it did and that it was a lie, except maybe if you were standing on the roof.

I took this in from outside the front gate while I waited to be let in. The cyclone fence around the place was perhaps three metres high with no razor wire, but I'd have bet on there being some kind of laser beam security. That's where the money was being spent. The entrance was a formidably electronic post and the guy inside the booth took his time looking at my credentials and communicating with what I'd come to think of as the Big House. It was a two-storey stucco affair, painted off-white and getting more that way. It had the look of a 1930s guesthouse that had been added to over the years. One of the additions was bars on some of the upstairs windows. A cyclone fence ran from both sides of the building to the wall. I could see figures moving around in the grounds behind it.

The guard returned my bits and pieces and the gate swung open. He stopped me as I drove through. 'Please keep all doors on the vehicle locked at all times and park in the marked spaces.'

I cruised the hundred or so metres along the thin-surfaced driveway and parked on a patch of cracked bitumen flanked by plane trees. From long habit I reversed into the space. Anyone who has ever done process serving knows to make arrangements for a quick getaway. It wasn't necessary here, but as I looked Rutherford House over from closer up it still seemed like a good idea. This was somewhere I'd want to get away from as quickly as possible.

Wide double doors led into a tiled lobby, converted by partitions into a reception area and a waiting room. A rather narrow and darkish corridor ran off into the bowels of the building. A staircase was roped off at the first landing. A receptionist in a uniform resembling a nurse's, but a bit more stylish, inspected my documents touching them as lightly as possible.

'Mr Harkness is being processed upstairs,' she said. 'Dr Whitfield will see you shortly in the waiting room.'

I took my time getting there. There were certificates and diplomas on the walls testifying to the expertise of the medical staff and the official standing of the institution. The only homey touch was a black-and-white photograph showing the place as it was fifty years back — the date had been written in the bottom left-hand corner in white ink. The building had one less wing and the bush pushed in closer at the back and sides. It looked a lot more friendly then than it did now. No bars, no cyclone fence.

After I'd sat for ten minutes or more in a less than comfortable chair a small, portly man in a white coat and dark trousers carrying a clipboard entered the waiting room. I shook his hand and, because he introduced himself as 'Dr Whitfield' and his white coat was buttoned all the way up I began to develop a dislike for him. His high, piping voice didn't help.

'Have you had any experience in dealing with people with psychosis, Mr Hardy?'

'I've had dealings with junkies, drunks, would-be suicides and actual murderers. Would that help?'

He looked at me sharply through his horn-rims and it was clear that the dislike was going to be mutual. 'Not quite what I meant. I take it you have no psychological training?'

'I did Psych I at UNSW a long time ago. It was all statistics so I dropped out.'

'Statistics are very important, very. But perhaps not to the point now. Mr Harkness suffers from a number of mental illnesses — manic depression, mild bi-polar disorder among them — all severely exacerbated by alcoholism.'

'But now he's cured, right?'

He ignored the question and signed a document on his clipboard. He detached it along with an envelope. He enclosed the document in the envelope and sealed it. 'Mr Harkness should present this to his therapist.'

'Who is?'

Ignoring questions was one of his little tricks. At least it spared me the reedy tones. He got up and clipped his gold pen into the breast pocket of his white coat. He wore a collar and tie under the coat and his black Oxfords were shiny. Maybe it was my old Italian slip-ons, drill slacks, open-neck shirt and unstructured linen jacket he didn't like, but somehow I feared it was just me. Still, I wasn't inclined to let him go just yet. I blocked his path to the door.

'Did you treat Harkness yourself?'

Not all small men are afraid of big men but those that are really are.

He retreated a half step. 'Myself and others.'

'Who does he contact here if he needs help? You?'

Somehow this seemed to give him courage. He let go a tight smile and slid around me. 'Mr Harkness won't apply here for help and I can't say I'm sorry. He'll be with you shortly.'

He scuttled away, ignoring the receptionist. I watched him disappear into the darkness and couldn't help thinking he was like one of the laboratory rats he had undoubtedly performed obscene experiments on. I remained standing at the waiting-room doorway and after a couple of minutes saw a man and a woman coming down the stairs. The woman unhooked the sash blocking the landing, patted the man on the shoulder, and he came down the rest of the way on his own.

At around 188 centimetres, Rodney Harkness held himself erect with his head well up. He didn't resemble either his mother or his brother. He was apparently in his late thirties but looked younger, with dark hair and a fresh complexion. With a weakish chin and a slightly crooked nose, he missed being handsome by a fair margin. He was the man I'd seen in the photograph with the woman and child, with a few more years and perhaps a broken nose added on. You wouldn't cast him as the lead — more the best friend type. His face was set in a determined expression; a mixture of hope and doubt. He was carrying a large overnight bag that, from the easy way he swung it as he reached the bottom of the stairs, was evidently nearly empty or he was a lot stronger than he looked. He stuffed an official-looking envelope in the pocket of his denim jacket and glanced quickly at the receptionist as if she might jump out and block his way.

I moved forward and tried to keep my voice neutral, non-custodial. 'Mr Harkness? My name's Cliff Hardy. I'm . . .'

'My nursemaid. I know. You can start earning your money by getting me the hell out of here.'

He stalked out and I followed him, closely

watching the way he moved. You can tell a lot about a person from the walk. Harkness moved athletically but with his free hand he tugged at the lapel of his jacket and the collar of his polo shirt. He wore jeans and sneakers and hitched at his belt several times over the short distance to the car. When we were out of the shadow of the building he lifted his head and gazed around, slowly taking in 180 degrees or more. Then he sucked in a deep breath as if savouring every cubic centimetre of free air. Or nearly free. When we got to the car, he dropped the bag, swivelled around and put out his hand.

'Sorry about that. I just couldn't believe I was actually getting out. Forgive the lousy manners.'

I shook his hand. 'It's okay,' I said. 'Cliff's the name in case you missed it.'

'Rod.' He looked at the car and smiled. 'I used to have one of these, except it had a roof-rack for my surfboard.'

I opened the door. He slung his bag into the back and settled into the seat. 'I'd ask you if I could drive except that I suppose my licence's expired.'

'That can be fixed.'

'Yeah, some things can be fixed and some can't. I've dreamed of this moment, Cliff. Forget what I said before — let's take it nice and slow.'

5

We negotiated the gates and he asked me to stop so he could take a look back at the place.

'I can't tell you how much I hated it,' he said. 'It was like a prison, for all the fancy psychobabble and bullshit.'

I nodded. 'I've been in prison. I can imagine.'

'Good. Something in common.' He picked up the case of the Ry Cooder tape and examined it. 'Yeah, he's good. D'you like Elvis?'

I'd got moving again but the question almost caused me to stall. 'What?'

'Elvis. D'you like him?'

'Sure, everyone on the planet likes Elvis . . . and the Beatles.'

'Elvis helped keep me sane. I'm full bottle on him. D'you know who did the originals of "That's All Right," "Mystery Train" and "Hound Dog"?'

'I suppose I thought "Hound Dog" *was* original Presley.'

'No. Arthur "Big Boy" Crudup, Junior Walker and Big Momma Thornton. I've read *Last Train to Memphis* and *Careless Love* four times. I've got 'em in the bag there. I'm going to throw them in the first fucking bin I see.'

'I wouldn't do that. The place they've got you is pretty spartan. A couple of books wouldn't go amiss.'

That quietened him. The institution was near the end of a road that wound around several large sections of bushland and rainforest somehow preserved from the developers. There was dense bush on both sides and ahead when I slowed to make a turn into the suburban road network. I had the window down and I heard the crack a microsecond before the windscreen exploded, showering us with glass. I ducked, grabbed Rod by the arm and pulled him down as I gunned the engine and swung the wheel to the left. The car jumped the gutter and I heard another shot ricochet off the roof as I slammed on the brake. Two cars at the intersection stopped and another pulled up behind us and everything went quiet.

I kept us down below the level of the shattered windscreen for a few seconds. I heard steps coming towards from behind and the sound of the cars at the intersection moving off. I lifted my head and let go Harkness's arm.

'Youse okay? What happened?'

It was the driver from behind who'd stopped like a good citizen. I opened the door and stepped out. 'We're okay. Thanks.'

'Jesus, you're bleeding.'

I lifted my hand to my face and felt the cuts. I turned back to Harkness, who was sitting up straight with all the colour drained from his face.

'Just some nicks,' I said to the samaritan. 'Must've been a stone.'

'Yeah, them old windscreens shatter like buggery. Well, if you're all right . . .'

'Thanks for stopping.' I turned back to Harkness. He was bleeding from cuts to his left ear and the side of his face. 'Pick the glass away carefully, bit by bit. Don't brush it.'

He did as I said and I did the same. Tiny cubes of glass lay all over the seat and floor. I opened the door and he got out and leaned against the car, sucking in deep breaths. 'That was no fucking stone.'

I reached into the back for a rag and brushed glass from the seat. 'No. Someone took a shot at us. Two shots. From over in the bush.'

'Shit. At me or you?'

'I can't think of anyone who'd want to kill me just at the moment.'

Colour was coming back into his face. I found a crumpled pack of tissues in the glove box and gave him a couple. We dabbed at our cuts while cars passed with their occupants looking at us curiously.

'You heard the shot and pulled me down,' Harkness said. He pushed back the hair that had flopped into his eyes and shoved the bloodied tissues into the pocket of his jacket.

'Reflex action,' I said. 'Let's find a garage and see if we can get the windscreen replaced.'

We got into the car and I reversed onto the road. The second bullet had left a long, raw scrape on the top of the Falcon.

'It's happened to you before, hasn't it. Cliff?'

'Broken windscreen? Sure.'

He laughed. 'Closest I've come to being shot at has been in television. They put in a windscreen made of a special sort of sugar and the armourer fires a blank charge.'

'I don't watch much television. What show was that?'

'It's a while back. I forget.'

I kept the speed down, but the breeze blowing into the car was still cool despite the mildness of the afternoon. At the second garage they said they could replace the windscreen, but not for a few days. The Falcon was too old for the size and shape to be in stock. The mechanic looked the car over doubtfully. 'Want the roof fixed, too?'

I said I did and he said it'd require a deposit so I let him take a swipe of the credit card. 'Gonna cost you.'

'That's life.'

I could see where the bullet had embedded itself in the upholstery at the back but I didn't think the windscreen repairer would notice; the back seat was pretty ratty anyway. We cleaned ourselves up in the station rest room. I phoned for a cab and we waited out front. There was a pub immediately across the highway and I could've done with a drink or two but it wasn't quite the time. Harkness hadn't said a word since mentioning his television work.

I unlocked the door to the Curlewis Street flat and watched Rod Harkness mooch in and drop his bag on the floor as if he'd occupied the place for years and it held no interest for him. He shrugged off his jacket and slung it on a chair, slumped into the nearest chair and barely cast a look around the living room. I went into the kitchen and saw that someone had paid a visit to the supermarket.

'They laid in some supplies for you,' I said. 'Want some coffee?'

He shrugged. 'Sure. Why not?'

'Sugar?'

'Three.'

I made two mugs of instant coffee and sat down across the room from him. 'We're going to have to talk. I was hired to keep an eye on you. Help you get back on your feet. There was nothing said about someone trying to kill you. I can usually read people pretty well, but I can't tell whether you're surprised or not. What're you feeling now — surprise, fear, don't-give-a-fuck — what?'

He stared at the brown carpet for a minute and then lifted his head slowly. Blood had started seeping from his cuts again and he'd touched them and smeared his face in spots. He had a tragic look that wasn't posed or theatrical. He took a long pull on his coffee and clasped his hands around the mug. 'To tell you the truth I think I'd describe my attitude as puzzled. Completely puzzled.'

I drank some coffee. Moccona freeze-dried, about the best instant you can get. There was blue-vein brie in the fridge along with olives and sweet and sour cucumbers. Two litres of milk, three bottles of Perrier, packets of sliced ham and smoked salmon. There was a loaf of rye bread and a bowl of fruit. I hadn't looked in the freezer compartment but I'd have been willing to bet it wasn't empty. The Harknesses hadn't abandoned the black sheep quite as thoroughly as I'd thought.

'Puzzled,' I said.

'Yeah. Do you know I've got no idea who's behind getting me out of Rutherford House? Every couple of years there'd be an examination and I'd be told I was staying a little longer. Then this last time . . . Jesus, I still can't quite believe it. Who . . .?'

'Didn't they tell you?'

'All I was told was that a firm of civil rights lawyers I've never heard of had instituted procedures that led to psychological assessments that advised my release. My fucking family appealed against the recommendation but the lawyers carried the day. I gather I'm sort of on probation and you're part of that, along with me taking my medication. And here we are.'

I felt a mild impulse to defend the family. 'Your family want to know who hired the lawyers as well.'

'I bet they do. But I don't suppose the lawyers are required to tell them.'

'I wouldn't know.' I took the credit card from my pocket and passed it across to him along with the documentation. 'They've provided you with funds.'

'How much?'

'Seven thousand bucks plus.'

'That's about right. I had a few grand left when I . . . I had to give Warren power of attorney.

Knowing him, he'd have invested it wisely. What else have they got in mind?'

I thought about it before replying. Should I tell him about his mother and brother commissioning Glen to find his wife and child? I decided to hedge the bet. 'Maybe you ought to ask them.'

He shook his head almost violently. 'No way. I couldn't bear to be in the company of either of them. Not for one minute. If you try to make me, I'll resist.'

I finished my coffee and made a don't-blame-me gesture with both hands. 'I'm not here to make you do anything.'

He grinned. 'No, you're here to stop me from drinking. Don't worry, I won't. The impulse has gone.'

'Good. That should make my job pretty easy.'

'I dunno about that.' He suddenly seemed to find some energy. He drained his mug, set it down on the floor, stood and began to inspect the flat. He went into the bedrooms, the bathroom, toilet and kitchen. I stood in the middle of the living room while he prowled around. He came from the kitchen munching on an apple.

'This isn't bad,' he said. 'What would it be worth, about?'

I shrugged. 'I don't know. Maybe six hundred thousand, maybe more.'

'Jesus. That much? I'm out of touch with property values along with everything else. Have I got a lease?'

'I saw an agent's card by the fruit bowl. You could ring them and find out.'

'Maybe you could ring them?'

'Look, Rod, I'm not your servant.'

'Sorry. I know that. I should have . . . You're a private detective, right?'

'Yes.'

'Okay. Well, I want to hire you to find how those lawyers who got me released found out about me and who's trying to kill me and if they're all one and the same.'

6

I phoned Glen, gave her the minimum amount of detail, and she said she'd be there inside an hour. I stalled Rod Harkness until then by telling him that I had to consult my partner. He occupied himself by going over the flat minutely, unpacking his bag and arranging his few belongings in the living room and the bedroom without the surfboard. He had a dozen or so books, including the two-volume biography of Elvis, and he arranged them on a shelf near the television.

He went into the other bedroom and stayed there for a few minutes. 'A Malibu,' he said as he came out. He lifted his eyebrows in the first theatrical gesture I'd seen from him.

'Good board,' I said.

'Old man's board — easy to paddle.'

When he opened the sliding door to step out onto the balcony I stopped him.

'Think,' I said. 'There'd be a dozen places around here to take a shot from.'

'Jesus. Am I going to have watch my back for the rest of my life? I feel like a protected witness.'

'Are you?'

'Am I what?'

'Are you a witness to something that someone doesn't want you talk about, ever?'

'No.' He closed the door and sat down. One hand felt the scratches on his face and ear, the other tapped nervously on the arm of the chair. 'What's he supposed to be doing, this partner of yours?'

'She. And I'll let her explain. More coffee?'

He nodded and I made some. I got out a mug for Glen and heard a knock at the door as I did so. I gestured to Harkness to be quiet and took a look through the spyhole. It was Glen looking stylish in a blue silk dress and tailored black jacket. I let her in.

'I hadn't necessarily planned to meet him,' she said quietly.

'What happened today changes things. He's in here. Want some coffee?'

'Okay.'

I filled the mugs. Harkness had his back to us and was looking out the window when we came into the room. I handed him a mug. 'This is Glen Withers, Rod. She's the enquiry agent your mother and brother hired. I'm sort of subcontracted to her.'

You see it sometimes but not often. An instant attraction between two people. A realisation hitting them both simultaneously that there's a connection between them, a set of possibilities. It comes out in the way they breathe, move and speak. It happened then. Glen and Rod transferred their coffee mugs to their left hands at the same time and shook hands as if the palms and fingers had been itching to meet. They didn't maintain the clasp for longer than was usual, but there was something reluctant in the way they broke the grip.

'Mr Harkness,' Glen said quietly. 'I'm glad to meet you.'

'Rod,' he said. 'Rod Harkness. Cliff and I are on first-name terms so I guess we should be.'

'Glen, then. Yes.'

They stood still, not far apart but apparently unable to move. I cleared my throat. 'Right. Let's sit down and thrash this out a bit.'

Glen moved to a chair and let her shoulder bag slide off. She caught it by the strap and lowered it to the floor. I sat down but Rod remained standing as if that was the best angle for him to look at her. He drank some coffee but it was just a way to stop himself from staring. She was expertly made up, her hair was shining and her clothes flattered her. I'd expected her to be in jeans and a T-shirt on a Sunday afternoon, the way she'd usually been when we were together, and wondered what she'd been doing. She drank some coffee and put the mug down on the floor beside her bag.

'How much have you told Rod about what we're doing?' Glen said. She was talking to me but she was glancing at him.

I shook my head. 'Virtually nothing.'

Glen shifted her sights firmly to Rod. 'That's how I was instructed to play it,' she said. 'I was to pursue my enquiries without meeting you or letting you know what I was doing. Cliff here was to help with your . . .'

Rod smiled. 'Rehabilitation.'

'If you like. But an attempt on your life changes things.'

Rod looked lost. 'How?'

'Someone got you out of Rutherford House,' I said. 'One of Glen's jobs was to find out who. If whoever got you out – I mean alerted the civil rights boys – did it in order to kill you then clearly Glen would be working in ignorance of all the circumstances. She *has* to know why you're a target.'

'But I've no idea.'

'That's why I have to tell you the rest of it, Rod,' Glen said. 'It's a relief in a way. I was never too happy working with a living, breathing human being as a sort of subject.'

I watched them both as she said that. One thing was sure — they weren't just subjects to each other now. I wondered if they sensed some sort of biochemical kinship, like the alcoholism. But it seemed unlikely. All I knew was I was beginning to get that three's-a-crowd feeling.

Rod drained his coffee mug and stretched. He did it easily and it was apparent that he hadn't just lain in bed for seven years. I seemed to recall from the website that there was a gym at Rutherford House, plus a tennis court and pool. 'So, Glen, what else are you investigating?'

Glen hesitated. 'I wonder if I should check with . . . my clients first. Tell them what's happened.'

'Only if you could do it face to face,' I said.

Rod and Glen both looked at me. Rod said, 'Why?' Glen said, 'You've lost me.'

'To get a read on their reactions. Isn't it possible

that there's really no mystery about who arranged for Rod's release? What if Rachel and Warren did it themselves? What if they want him dead?' I waved my hand at the flat, including Glen and myself. 'What if all this's just an elaborate cover?'

'That'd be diabolical,' Rod said.

'Are you saying they're not?'

Rod didn't answer.

Glen's coffee was down to the dregs and she swilled them the way a Scotch drinker swills the last bit of liquor and the remnant of the ice trying to make it last, wishing there was more. 'It would also be highly insulting. They'd be betting I couldn't find that out.'

I shrugged. 'They don't know how good you are.'

'I'm getting lost here,' Rod said. 'Please tell me what else you were supposed to investigate. If it's necessary you can still brace Warren and my mother about the shooting and see how they react.'

'That's true,' I said.

Glen drew in a deep breath. 'Okay. The other part of my commission was to attempt to locate your wife and child. Your mother and brother said they hoped to reunite you with your daughter.'

Neither Glen nor I was in any way ready for what happened next. Rodney Harkness seemed to shrink in size as if he was cringing away from his physical existence. He let out a high-pitched shriek, sprang from his chair and dashed to the bedroom. He slammed the door and Glen and I sat there and listened to his passionate and despairing keening.

7

When the sound of Rod's distress reached an unbearable level, Glen got up and went into the bedroom, closing the door behind her. I heard murmurs and the wailing broke down into sobs and then sniffs and then silence. I wandered around the flat wishing, illogically, that there was something strong to drink. I flicked through a couple of Rod's books, including the Presley biographies. The little bits I read confirmed my impression that Elvis was a deeply needy man who was ruthlessly exploited. But then, as a friend of mine once said to someone who'd put this proposition in a pub discussion, 'He spread 'em.'

I inspected the surfboard again. The receipt had gone. A lot of work to wax. Just the thought of paddling it out to catch the waves made my shoulders ache. If Rod was going to take up surfing again he'd do it with me on the beach. That thought jerked me back to what I should have been thinking about all along: Minding him had turned into protecting him and protecting him logically led to finding out who wanted to kill him, which was what he was offering to hire me to do.

Given my contract with Glen, not to mention our association, how awkward was that?

Although it had been spelled out in the information we'd already been given, one thing was now even clearer than before — judging by his reaction to Glen's talk of finding his wife and child, their loss was at the heart of his problems. Glen emerged as I was unenthusiastically contemplating another coffee.

'He's exhausted,' she said. 'Probably sleep for a while. You making more coffee?'

We took the mugs out on to the balcony. If there was someone holding money to kill Harkness and expecting more, he wouldn't take pot shots at two non-targets. I was sure from watching from the taxi that Rod and I hadn't been followed to Bondi, but that raised the question of how many people knew about the flat.

'You'll have to find out from your clients who knows about Rod being here,' I said. 'So we can judge how safe he is.'

'Right. My impression is that Warren handled it, but who knows? He might have put his secretary on it. Think I should tell them what's happened, Cliff?'

'Tricky. And here's another one. He,' I inclined my head towards the bedroom, 'tried to hire me to find out who wants him dead.'

'Shit. What did you say?'

'Said I'd talk to you.'

'This has got stickier than it started out, and it was sticky enough.'

'And how.'

Glen raised an eyebrow. 'That doesn't sound like you. What does that mean?'

I meant, *and you're attracted to him*, but I said, 'Nothing. I think we're going to have to work more closely together on this than we thought.'

'You're staying with it though, aren't you? Even though minding isn't protecting.'

She had a double need now — the need to be working, to be engaged, and the interest in Harkness himself. 'Sure,' I said. 'Might have to vary the contract a bit. Expenses'll be higher.'

'Thanks, Cliff. I think we'll split it down the middle. I'll look for the wife and child and you find out who's trying to kill him. That gives you the pointy end.'

'Only right. What about finding who's behind getting him out?'

Neither of us had touched our coffee and it was cold by now. Glen emptied hers out into a pot plant holding a stunted rubber tree and I followed suit. 'I think we might both be involved in that one,' she said.

We put off talking about Rod's collapse and what it might mean for his fitness to get on with his life. Instead we discussed whether or not to tell Lady Rachel and Warren about the shooting.

'It could have just been some crazy. Pot-shotting,' Glen said.

'Two shots, well grouped, from concealment. Quick exit. I don't think so.'

'Someone after you?'

'Can't think of anyone just at the present. Not likely to either.'

'Okay. Let's be practical. Will telling them make our jobs easier or harder?'

I considered. 'Easier, maybe. Sit Warren down. Tell him. Ask him if he knows of anyone who had it in for Rod that much. He might have made all sorts of enemies, who knows?'

'What about her?'

I shrugged. 'Leave her in the dark. Divide and rule. Let Warren decide whether to tell her or not.'

'I like it.'

'So, have you made a start on tracking the wife?'

'Yes. I'm running credit checks on her under her unmarried and married names. Car registration. All that. Plus I've got a contact in Immigration checking women leaving the country around the time of the last letter. Her father's dead; mother could be alive and I'm looking. Plus she had a brother and I'm looking for him, too. Warren says there was a missing person report filed and I'm trying to get the file on that from the police. That sound all right to you?'

'Sure. Can I get copies of these letters she wrote to Rod?'

'I suppose. Why?'

'Just to be up to speed. Another thing, when I dig the bullet out of the back seat of my car, can you get it appraised for me? You've got the contacts.'

'All right.'

I felt I couldn't avoid the question any longer. 'What medication is he on?'

'Didn't they tell you at the institution?'

'They told me bugger-all and the little prick who was releasing him had a Gestapo look to him. Hang on.' I got up and took Rod's jacket from the chair where he'd dropped it. The long envelope wasn't sealed and I opened it and took out some papers.

Glen gave the closed door a quick look and then joined me in inspecting the papers. There was a form for his release on the court order, several documents from Rutherford House indicating dates of review of his case and a certified copy of a statement by a Dr Jerry Weir advising that Harkness was fit to rejoin society. There was a list of recommended therapists. Nothing about medication. Maybe Rutherford House was wary about revealing what he'd been on.

'I think I might have a talk to this Dr Weir,' I said. 'He seems to be one of the good guys.'

'A shrink. He won't tell you anything.'

'You never know. Meanwhile I suppose I'd better stay here tonight and keep an eye on him. Though we're going to have to give him some time on his own if we're going to do any useful investigating.'

'Yeah, but not right away.'

'No, I'll stick close for a couple of days at least, but I need to nip out now for a few minutes.'

'Why?'

'I have to get something to drink.'

'Right.'

'Do you mind waiting, or are you going out somewhere?'

'No. Why?'

'You're all dressed up?'

She delayed answering by carefully folding up the papers and restoring them to the envelope and the jacket. She kept her head turned away. 'I do it from time to time to make me feel better.'

Over the next few days I did what I'd been expecting to do with Rodney Harkness, which was hang out with him. He seemed to recover from his fugue and made no reference to it the next day. We stayed local. Bondi. Bondi Junction. Nothing fell from a great height. No drive-by shooting. He drew out some money and shopped for food, things for the flat and some clothes. He bought some expensive coffee and a top-line grinder, ground it himself and drank quite a lot of it. If he was missing the grog he didn't show it. It turned out that he could cook and he did and seemed to enjoy it. He joined the Waverley Library and borrowed some books, mostly biographies.

He asked me a few questions about Glen and I filled him in as much as I thought necessary.

'Were you on with her?'

'For a time. Quite a while ago. It ended amicably, more or less.'

I didn't tell him about her drinking or AA. Her business. The third day I left him at a movie and checked my messages at home and at the office. Glen left a message to say that Warren had arranged the flat and bank account himself and that no-one else knew about it. She'd got Warren to phone Rutherford House and he'd been told that Rod wasn't on any medication. Nothing else important except that the car was ready. In the afternoon we got a bus up to the northern beaches and collected the car. They'd done a good job on the roof and the windscreen and there didn't seem to be any glass inside the car. But there would be; there always is.

He was quiet as we began the drive back, taking in the sights. Around Mona Vale he stopped looking and turned his head towards me. 'Are you going to let me hire you, Cliff?'

'It's dodgy. I've talked about it to Glen because I'm sort of subcontracted to her. Why don't we let it ride for a while? See how it works out. But since I'm going to try and find out who worked on your release . . . you know, one thing could lead to another.'

'How are you going to go about that? They wouldn't tell me. That is, they wouldn't say who brought my case to the attention of the lawyers.'

I didn't want to set him off again by saying I'd talk to the shrink. I told him I'd get some legal advice about accessing the Rutherford House records. I suggested that if the worst came to the worst they could be hacked into. Gave him some mumbo-jumbo about Freedom of Information. He seemed to swallow it.

'I should be thinking about getting back to work,' he said. 'Getting my life in order. But with this life threat stuff, and not knowing who's fucking with me . . . it's hard to focus on it.'

Safe train of thought. Worth encouraging. 'Will you try acting again?'

'Maybe. Or writing. I saw some weird things in that place. I might try a film script, couldn't be worse than some of the shit that gets out. I'd have to get an agent of course. Jesus!'

'What?'

'No, he wouldn't. Not even that mad bastard'd do that.'

'What're you talking about?'

'I've just remembered. I had this agent, Doug Schirer. Bloody hopeless. I reckon he lost me more jobs than he got me by being such a smart-arse. Eventually I told him I was dropping him and then I lucked onto a good thing in a series of commercials. Shit, I got it myself. He didn't have anything to do with it. Good money. Residuals, you know? He claimed his commission and I told him to get fucked. This was . . . before. He went under soon after and he said it was my fault, that I'd robbed him of a commission that would've kept him afloat and that I'd bad-mouthed him in the trade. I hadn't. Well, maybe I had, a bit. He said he'd get even with me.'

I shook my head sceptically. 'Come on. Seven years ago, Rod. Not very likely.'

'Yeah, I know. But the thing is, his hobby was shooting. Bloody Doug was a crack shot, nearly made it to the Olympics.'

I was only half paying attention to what he was saying because I'd begun to get an uneasy feeling from watching the ebb and flow of traffic in the rear vision mirror. I'd had the feeling before, more than a few times, and it usually means something. I wasn't sure and I'd have to perform a few manoeuvres to find out, but I had a strong suspicion that we were being followed.

8

'Don't look round,' I said.

'Why not?'

'I don't want him to know I'm onto him. I have to think what to do.'

We were approaching Narrabeen in moderate traffic. The lightness of the traffic had helped me spot the tail. An off-white 4WD. That, and the fact that the driver wasn't first class at the job. The 4WD stayed well back but had changed lanes when I had capriciously, and when I slowed for no good reason it'd slowed as well. A couple of times it would have been logical for the driver to have passed other vehicles. Didn't happen.

Rod sat silent for a while, then he drew in a deep breath and spoke hesitantly. 'This is weird. Art and life, you know? I've played this scene a couple of times. You know what happened? I was a spy, like an ASIO agent, and I sort of lured the car following me into a place where I could surprise him. It worked okay on TV.'

'This isn't a film and I'm not going to do anything like that.'

'Why not?'

I concentrated on my driving for a while as I thought it through. 'It's a big four-wheel-drive, newish, a Santa Fe, something like that.'

'I can't tell one of those things from another, never could.'

'Glen's got a Pajero. I've driven it a few times and liked it. I was thinking of getting something like that. I looked at a few. The thing is, I can't see how many people are in it. Tinted glass.'

'So you don't like the odds?'

'I don't like not knowing. I don't like the odds if there's more than one and if one of them's got that fucking rifle.'

'Haven't you got a gun?'

'Not with me.'

'So what're the options?'

'Hang on. I'm trying to get the number. Shit, it's smeared over. This isn't a game. Have you got any other ideas?'

'I suppose we could ram it.'

'Yeah, send it rolling through the guard rail so it bursts into flames and we drive on. End of problem.'

'I wasn't being serious.'

'Okay. Sorry. The only thing we can do is lose him.'

'Or her. You said your friend Glen drove one.'

Fuck you, I thought. 'Okay. My guess is we're being followed to find out where you're living. Poor bugger's been staking out that garage since Sunday. If we lose him or her it's a win.'

'I thought you said it wasn't a game.'

One to him. I didn't reply, trying to work out a

strategy. Not too hard. I tooled along down to Brookvale, showing every sign of intending to stay on Pittwater Road to Manly. But before the fork with Condamine Street I edged over, crossed a line of traffic and took the Harbord turn-off to the east. The Santa Fe, if that's what it was, was committed to Pittwater Road and there was no way I was going to let it pick me up again.

'That was slick,' Rod said.

'Thanks. At least we've learned that whoever's after you isn't tied in to your brother and mother.'

'How do you figure that?'

'They're looking for you. If they were tied in they'd already know. So it looks like you're safe in Bondi for now.'

'I can't stay in Bondi for the rest of my life.'

'No, but you can for a while. Get on that Malibu.'

I drove on, working my way back to where I wanted to be and keeping a weather eye open. I ran my mind back over all I could remember of what had been said to who by whom since this business began. Something jumped into my head.

'What was all that about your agent?'

I circled the block several times before deciding that it was safe to park at the flat. Rod Harkness was bearing up well under the pressure of being shot at and tracked. He seemed to be able to put such things aside and get on with his reading and cooking. He went out briefly around six o'clock and I thought, *Uh oh, happy hour.* But he came back with a yellow legal pad and spent a good bit of the next hour writing on the table in the living room. It was me who went out for a couple of drinks after his passable veal stroganoff.

I sat in the bar of the Bondi Hotel watching the black and white Kiwis mix with the black and white Australians. You could distinguish them pretty well by their T-shirts — 'All Blacks', 'Wallabies', 'Sheep Fuckers', 'Warriors', although there were probably some crossovers. They drank and played darts and pool and got on well for the most part under the great comradely influence of beer and tobacco. I nursed a couple of Scotches and thought over what Rod had told me about his ex-agent, Doug Schirer.

'It ended in a stand-up fight,' Rod had said. 'And I decked him. I was pissed of course, and Doug was a mad cokehead in those days. It was crazy, but there was a lot of money involved. And with residuals you can go on earning good dough for years if the commercial gets a long run and revivals.'

'Did yours?' I asked.

Rod shrugged. 'I dunno. Everything went to shit after that and I . . .'

He stopped there and I didn't press him, not wanting to push him towards the brink again. Then he got stuck into his writing and I let it slide. But I had a few more questions in mind and thought it might be safe to put them when I got back. I'd sneaked a look at his pad when he went for a piss. He was writing a script about a wife who left her husband. *Okay*, I thought, *let's hope writing's as cathartic as they say it is.*

On my return, Rod glanced up from his pad and grinned at me. He looked the happiest I'd seen him. 'You don't have to do that, you know.'

'Do what?'

'Sneak out for a drink. I wouldn't mind if you had a slab in the fridge and a case of Johnny Walker in your room.'

'Better safe than sorry. But are you really that clear of it?'

'I think so. Seven years. Well, no. There was that time early on, Buster Lewis got a couple of bottles smuggled in and then again when Luigi Coppola cooked up some grappa. But otherwise, yeah.'

'Good for you. How's the writing going?'

'It's fun. I think I might get a cheap computer and that scriptwriting software.'

'You know about that stuff?'

He smiled. 'I read a lot of magazines in there. Had the time.'

He'd made another pot of his premium coffee and I put a mug of it in the microwave and got it hot. I sat down across the table from him. 'Okay, a couple of questions.'

'Alcohol's good for stimulating questions. So's tobacco. I can smell public bar on you, Cliff.'

'Shit, you're not a recovering smoker, too?'

'No. I never smoked except phoney cigarettes on the set.'

'You're lucky, mate, I did. Just supposing your commercial's gone on earning big bucks. Who'd be getting the money?'

'It's not likely but with everything that's happened I haven't even thought about it. I suppose it'd be going to Barney Nugent who was my agent when . . . You know.'

'You haven't heard from him?'

'No. But I'd better get in touch if this comes to anything.' He gestured at the pad.

'What was the commercial for?'

'Olympic running shoes. I was the winged god Mercury who gave the shoes to the black kid. I mean it was sentimental crap. Olympic's like all the rest — uses Asian sweated labour — but actors can't be choosers.'

'I've seen that one,' I said. 'It's been on a lot — world championships, Commonwealth Games. It got a big run around the time of the Sydney games. You couldn't turn on the TV without seeing it. There must be a fair bit in the kitty for you, depending on the contract.'

Rod shook his head. 'I can't remember much about it but I was strong on the residuals. Sometimes they cut out after a couple of repeats but I think I held out for more than that.'

'It sounds like we'd better have a word with both these blokes. One could have it in for you for diddling him out of the money and the other one might not want to hand over what he's got. Are these agents generally honest?'

Rod grinned. 'When it suits them. But it couldn't be enough money to kill for.'

'How much is that? It varies. What if Barney's spent it all on blondes and horses?'

Rod laughed. 'No way. Barney's a pussycat. Doug's another matter. He's an ex policeman and . . .'

'That means he could've had a way of finding when you were getting out. What if Doug's in it with Barney?'

Rod scribbled something on his pad. 'Good plot point,' he said.

'What?'

'Never mind. So we talk to them, do we? We can look them up in the phone book. What's that you've got?'

On the way back from the pub I'd opened the car and dug the rifle bullet out of the back seat with my Swiss army knife. I put it on the table and spun it. 'It'll have rifling marks on it that can identify the weapon that fired it.'

'Can you tell what sort of bullet it is?'

'Not me, but I know people who can. Glen for one. She did a course on it.' Mention of Glen set him doodling on his pad. I located the phone directories and looked up Agents — Theatrical. Barney Nugent was there with an address in Paddington but there was no sign of Doug Schirer.

Rod had gone back to his writing.

'Did this Schirer have a company name?' I asked. 'Olivier Theatrical Agency, something like that?'

Rod barely glanced up. 'Doug? No chance. Too egotistical.' He scribbled a bit more and then put his pen down. 'Sorry. I'm not helping, am I? It's just that writing feels like a bloody good thing to do. Better than that bullshit therapy back at Rutherford. Okay, Doug. He got into it when he was hired as a consultant for a TV doco on police corruption. He reckoned he was ripped off. He claimed that he coached the actors for the reconstruction scenes, bloody near wrote the script and told the director what to do. Maybe he did. It happens. Anyway, there was a fair bit of that sort of work around at the time — '60 Minutes', crimestopper stuff, you know? Doug edged his way in. He had some ex-coppers on his books and ex-crims like Billy Parkinson who'd taken up acting and writing. Did you look up literary agents as well?'

I hadn't. I did. Still no Schirer.

Rod was into the full flood of memory now. He microwaved coffee for both of us and stabbed at his pad with his pen. 'I went with Doug because that was the sort of stuff I was getting work in around the time — cop shows, pilots and such, and he was aggressive. He got me a few things and took his full whack, let me tell you. Twenty per cent. That was all right. Then the money got to him. He started hanging around with the really big earners and he got on the coke and he was fucking hopeless. Mind you, I was well on the way to being hopeless myself.'

This was dangerous ground after the performance of a few days back but I risked it. 'How d'you mean?'

'Lucille and I weren't getting on. I was drinking too much. Did you have another question?'

Not bad, I thought. *He handled that moment pretty well.* I asked some meaningless question, got a reply and then he went back to his writing. I sipped the hot coffee and wished I'd had another drink. The flat was well insulated, double-glazed and there was nothing to be heard except the scratch of Rod's pen, so the sudden ringing of the phone startled us both.

'Who's got the number?' Rod said.

I considered. 'Your brother, I guess. And Glen.'

'I don't want to talk to Warren.'

I nodded and picked up the phone.

'Cliff? It's Frank Parker.'

I'd forgotten that I'd given Frank the number. When I said his name Rod looked at me enquiringly. 'It's all right,' I said.

Frank sounded puzzled. 'What's all right?'

'I'm talking to someone else, Frank. What's new?'

'I've got the name of the detective who arrested Rodney Harkness and interviewed him. He's retired. I've had a word with him and he says he'll talk to you. I'll give you the details.'

'Great.' I pulled out my notebook and a pen and scribbled down the name and address.

'He's a good bloke,' Frank said. 'He retired on a disability pension. Took a bullet in a bank hold-up. He seems to remember Harkness pretty clearly so there must be something noteworthy about it.'

I thanked him and then had a thought. 'Not wanting to lay too much on you, but do you know anything about a former member of the force named Doug Schirer?'

Rod was staring at me now and the silence at the other end of the line was heavy. Eventually Frank said, 'Do I ever. He's involved, is he?'

'Could be.'

'That's bad news. He's a real bastard, Cliff. Got

kicked out for corruption and brutality. No, I think he resigned before he could be kicked out. Then he had something to do with television.'

'That's him. Do you know what he's doing now?'

'Don't you?'

'No, I never heard of him until just lately. What do you mean?'

'I've no idea how it happened but somehow he got a private enquiry licence. He's a member of your bloody profession, Cliff. That is, nominally.'

'Meaning?'

'The word is he's been a hit man in his time. A pricey one.'

9

I figured to spend a few more days making sure Rod was settled in and on the straight and narrow before taking a look at Doug Schirer and Barney Nugent. When I checked with Glen she said she'd established that Lucille Hammond and her daughter hadn't left Australia around the time specified.

'That's unless they had false passports, credit cards in another name and such,' Glen said. 'Which doesn't seem likely. Don't think she'd have known how to go about it. She seems to have been a handful and not very bright.'

'What did she do before she got married?'

'Aerobics instructor — a gym bunny, starving herself and exercising her tits off, literally. Apparently she had a hard time giving birth and suffered a bit of post-natal depression.'

We were in a coffee bar opposite the computer store where Rod was buying his machine. He'd consulted with Glen about the purchase, listened intently to her advice, but insisted on doing the buying himself.

'A good sign, that,' Glen had said. 'Wants to make his own decisions. A lot of recovering drunks become completely dependent. They substitute one addiction for another.'

'And how are you doing?'

She flapped her hand noncommittally. 'So-so. Have you told him about me?'

'No. Why would I do that?'

'Never mind. Anyway, I'm waiting to hear back on the bank and credit and car registration enquiries. If they turn up blank then she's really gone to ground.'

I told Glen about the possibility of there being money held in trust for Rod from his TV commercial. Glen looked thoughtful. 'Lucille didn't have any money of her own as far as I can see. Warren says she made no approaches to him. And there's the kid to support. Did Rod make this commercial before the break-up?'

'I think so, yes.'

'Then she must have known about it. It's strange she didn't look for support. File for divorce. She'd have walked it in. Got child support, custody, the lot.'

Rod emerged from the shop and crossed the street looking pleased with himself. He waylaid a waiter and ordered more coffee. 'An iMac,' he said as he plonked himself down. 'As you recommended. Laser printer and a scanner. Plus I've put in an order for the software. There's only one thing.'

Glen leaned forward. 'What?'

Rod grinned. 'I've never used a computer. Wouldn't have a clue how to fly one.'

'I'll show you,' Glen said.

The computer would be arriving the next day and they made an arrangement to have a training session. Glen went off about her business and Rod said it was time for him to try the surfboard. He was energetic, jumping out of his skin, and I knew enough about rehabilitation to know that it was a dangerous state. Hyper up can lead to hyper down and listening to the siren call of booze or drugs. A good dose of surf exhaustion could be just the ticket. We headed down to the beach, Rod in his new boardies and wetsuit vest, and me in jeans, sneakers and a T-shirt with the Chow Hayes book, a peaked cap, shades, sunblock and two cans of light beer in a plastic bag.

It had turned into one of those days Sydney can supply at almost any time of the year. The sky was clear and the breeze was light with no bite to it. The water was an intense, sparkling blue and the breaking waves were a laundry detergent seller's dream. I knew that the water contained concentrations of chemicals unknown in Sir Joseph Banks' time, and that the air held particles toxic to human tissue. But that was laboratory stuff. To the naked eye, Bondi Beach was perfect.

'South end I think,' Rod said. 'Waves look better. More of a challenge.'

'If you say so.'

We walked along the concourse and down steps to the sand. The place had changed a little in recent times although the stadium erected for the Olympics beach volleyball seemed to have left no scars. A new lifesaver lookout post being built on the concourse was a bit of an eyesore and the post-mounted rubbish bins on the beach were an innovation, probably necessary. The rails that ran around the concourse had rusted out and been removed sometime in the seventies if my memory served. Now they were back. I found a spot, scooped up sand for a backrest and lowered myself. Rod dropped his towel, kicked off his sandals and trotted down to the water with the big board firmly in his grasp. He went in without hesitation, waded to waist deep, straddled the board and started paddling. Paddling a surfboard looks easy but isn't, and just about anyone who tries for the first time falls off. Again, for a novice, the arm and shoulder muscles start to hurt after fifty metres. Rod Harkness didn't fall off and he looked as if he could just about take the thing halfway to New Zealand. He reached the breakers very quickly, well before two other surfers who'd started out at about the same time.

I put on my sunglasses against the glare and squinted. There he was in classic mode, bobbing in the swell, looking back to read the waves with an occasional sidelong glance to monitor the traffic. It made me remember my surfing youth at Maroubra when I'd spent hours in the water risking skin cancer and shark bite and paraplegia, all things that happened to other people. In a way I envied the aging rock stars who flew their helicopters and the middle-aged journalists who went on smoking thirty a day as if it couldn't happen to them. I knew that it could.

A decent wave built up behind Rod and he propelled his board forward, caught it at the first strong movement of the water, and stood up. Immediately, he lost balance and fell off. Neatly, though, and he was back up and paddling out again before another two waves had passed him. I found myself hoping he'd catch the next one and he did. Whatever wrong move he'd made on the first wave he eliminated, and he rode this one conservatively but with a lot of skill until it carried him to every last metre of its energy. A confidence builder.

I watched him ride another couple and then turned my attention to the beach. Nothing suspicious in sight. I read a few pages about the old gunman who, to judge by the photographs, spent his whole time, summer and winter, in a suit, collar and tie with hat. Did no work on Bondi Beach. I yawned, cracked a can and drank it slowly. Nice work if you can get it. I read a bit more and then looked up to see Rod ride a long, curling one right into the shallows. He slipped from the board and undid his leg rope. He lifted the board clear and left the water. He waded ashore and raised his fist in a triumphant salute.

As he was trotting up the sand, a man who was adjusting his balls inside his togs blundered into Rod's path and caused him to lose balance and drop the board.

I watched lazily until I saw Rod pick up the board and swing it hard against the man's back. He went down and I was up and running towards them. The man was big and well-built but quick on his feet. He sprang up and moved aggressively forward, well balanced. Rod jabbed the board hard into his chest and the man went down again. He was a street fighter. He scooped up sand, threw it at Rod's face and came in low, bullocking. Rod dropped the board and waited for him.

The question that was skipping in my brain as I raced across the sand, dodging people and trying to keep my balance was, *Is this it?* I had almost reached the pair as Rod misjudged the force of his opponent's rush and the level of his head. He took a heavy butt to the mid-section, lost his footing and went down. Then the man made the mistake of swinging a foot at Rod's head. A bare-foot kick won't hurt much unless delivered by an expert, which this guy wasn't. Rod was adrenalin-pumped. He took the blow, grabbed the foot and twisted. The man roared in pain and went down on his knees as Rod got quickly to his feet. He drove a knee into the guy's face, held him by the hair and got into position to deliver a karate chop. I grabbed his forearm and stopped the swing. Rod struggled; he was stronger than me but unbalanced and I held him there long enough.

'Stop it, you bloody idiot,' I hissed in his face. 'Pick up that fucking board and let's get out of here.'

His eyes were starting from his head and a vein was throbbing in his temple. I bore down on his arm, locking it against his body. He sucked in a breath and the force seemed to go out of him.

'Okay, okay,' he said.

I let him go. People had gathered to watch the fight, but at a respectable distance. Rod and I avoided eye contact with them and the man he'd beaten. He was still on his knees with blood dripping from his nose to the sand, but he didn't seem to be seriously hurt. Rod picked up his board and we moved back up the beach.

'Jeez,' I heard one of the spectators say, 'that guy's got a murderous temper.'

I collected my things and Rod's sandals and stuffed them into the bag. Rod was standing and looking down at the sand, breathing hard. I threw his towel at him and he fumbled the catch. He looked diminished and afraid, nothing like the athlete who'd ridden the waves so triumphantly. 'Let's go.'

He looked at me and his eyes had lost their fire and were soft and pleading. I almost felt sorry for him. 'Did you think it was another serious go at you?'

He shook his head. 'No. I just lost my block. But you're supposed to be on my side.'

I shoved at his shoulder and got him moving. 'I am,' I said. 'Maybe you'd have liked being charged with assault. That'd put you back in Rutherford House faster than you can shit.'

He plodded across the sand with his shoulders slumped like a schoolboy caught shoplifting and going home to tell his mum. 'I didn't take the Valium this morning,' he said. 'I felt good and didn't think I needed it. Not a good idea in the surf anyway.'

We reached the concourse and I directed him to a shower. He was obedient. He washed the sand from his legs and back. Then he rinsed down the board and the leg rope. He seemed childishly pleased to have these tasks to perform. I sneaked a look back at the beach, where the disturbance caused by the fight seemed to have faded away. Lucky. If there'd been an inspector around or some officious type with a mobile phone . . .

When he was dry I gave him his sandals. 'They never told us what medication you were on.'

'Just Valium.'

Just Valium, I thought. *Great.* And *without it* . . .? I couldn't count the number of mood swings I'd seen courtesy of Valium. The comment from the beach hit me again: *That guy's got a murderous temper.*

10

The computer arrived at ten the next morning and Glen showed up soon after to give Rod his lesson. He hadn't said a word about the fight on the beach and seemed to have forgotten all about it, perhaps in the excitement of getting the computer. When we had a moment alone as he was unpacking the thing she handed me an envelope.

'Copies of the wife's letters.'

I pocketed the envelope. 'Looked at by whom?'

She spoke, quoting, 'Police experts confirmed that they were in the hand of Mrs Lucille Harkness and written in a state of extreme distress.'

'As you'd expect. Have you turned up anything else?'

'Some stuff about her. Bit of a good-time girl, apparently.'

'Okay, here's something for you.' I gave her the bullet. 'Dug out of the upholstery of my car. As I said, I thought you could use your old contacts to find out a bit about it.'

'Why're you being so shitty?'

'What?'

'You know. I can feel the chill coming off you.'

I wanted to tell her what I'd seen on the beach and about the Valium and the misgivings I was starting to entertain about Rod, but I didn't. I hadn't the heart. She was smartly turned out again though less formal than last time. Her hair gleamed; her clothes became her; she smelled good, but it was more a matter of the way she moved and the gestures she made. A survivor of a few relationships, I knew the signs. No matter how intelligent and wary, a woman who's interested in a man gives off certain vibes. The object of her affection may not pick them up but an observer, especially a slightly jealous one, can.

'Sorry,' I said. 'It's nothing. I'm off to see this bloke who may possibly have been the shooter and . . .'

'You didn't tell me about this.'

I grabbed my keys. 'No time. Rod'll fill you in.'

Glen put the bullet in the pocket of her pink linen jacket. 'I'm right. You are shitty,' she said.

Douglas A. Schirer, PEA, advertising himself in the Yellow Pages as 'former NSW Police Service senior detective — 3 citations for meritorious action' plus 'discreet and hi-tech enquiries', had an office on the Great Western Highway in Five Dock. Not far to go. But Doug's ad included his phone number, fax number, mobile number and email address. After getting back from the beach yesterday and seeing Rod off to a late afternoon nap thanks to his Valium, I'd rung the phone numbers and been shunted from one to the other. Then I went to an Internet café and sent Schirer a message suggesting a meeting to discuss a professional matter. He also had a website with his photograph — wavy hair grey at the temples with the regulation copper's bristly moustache, also with a touch of grey. Hard to judge from a head and shoulders shot, but he seemed to be on the large side; he hailed from the era when there was a height requirement for police. Now I was on my way back to my office to check the state of play generally with my business, but mostly to see if Doug had responded.

Darlinghurst changes only subtly, a touch here and a touch there. The email addresses and websites have sprouted on every second shop front and I fancied there were a few more fetish clothing stores in recent times. The street people cleared away for the Olympics were back, perhaps in greater numbers. It was said that the safe injecting room had cut down on street shooting-up but I hadn't been to that end of the Cross lately to find out. St Peters Lane, which my building backs onto, gets a clean-up from time to time but the old look — cardboard boxes, discarded implements, broken plastic milk crates — always creeps back in.

I went up to the office, checked the answering machine and fax and found nothing important pending. I made a cup of instant coffee and sat down at the computer. While I waited for it to boot up, I examined Lucille Harkness's letters.

Rodney
I can't take any more. I'm leaving with Rose. Please don't try to stop me.
Lucille

Rodney
I know you've been trying to find me. I told you not to and I mean it.
Lucille

Rodney
Don't make me hate you. Please. Please. Please.
L

Rodney Harkness
It's no good. You'll never understand. I'm sorry but there's nothing left.
L

The script was loopy, almost childlike, and the pressure on the ballpoint pen had varied almost from word to word. The last letter in particular was written in something between script and the printing of individual letters as if the writer was ready to stop at any time. If the police expert said this was evidence of extreme distress I was ready to believe it.

I folded the letters and put them in a folder with the copy of the contract I'd signed with Glen and the other papers she'd provided. The photographs of Lucille Hammond and Rose Harkness I kept tucked inside my notebook. I turned my attention to the computer and logged on for my email. Along with a routine message from the server, one from the bank about getting online and one from my accountant suggesting that I make an appointment to see him to discuss my GST obligations, there was one from Schirer sent in the early hours of the morning:

Hardy
Heard of you. I'll be in the office for half an hour around 1 pm today.

The man worked long hours. I tapped out a reply that I'd be there, ignored the other messages and logged off. I had some time to kill so I looked up the document from Dr Jerry Weir, the psychiatrist. The address was a clinic in Mosman. I read recently that the mean price for a house in the suburb was now over a million dollars. Good place to do business. I rang the number and asked to be put through to Dr Weir.

'What is it concerning?' the receptionist asked.

'A patient.'

'Are you a practitioner?'

Sure, I thought. 'A consultant.'

A short pause and then a cool female voice came on the line. 'This is Jerry Weir. Who am I speaking to?'

I tried to keep the unjustified surprise out of my voice. 'My name's Hardy, Dr Weir. I'm a private investigator. I understand you gave an opinion recently regarding a Mr Rodney Harkness.'

I don't know whether or not I controlled my surprise but she certainly didn't. 'Rodney? Yes, I did. Why, what's happened to him?'

Rodney?

'Do you expect something to happen?'

'Mr . . . Hardy, was it? I don't think I can discuss a case over the telephone.'

'That's right. Could we meet?'

'I don't know. This is most unusual.'

'So's Rodney Harkness. It's important that I talk to you.'

'There's very little I can say.'

That wasn't what she meant at all. She just needed another gentle push. 'A number of disturbing things have happened, doctor. I'd greatly value your opinion on some of the things that've been said and done regarding Mr Harkness.'

'That's very shrewdly put, Mr Hardy. All right, I suppose I could see you. When do you suggest?'

I told her I had an appointment in the early part of the afternoon and suggested that I come to Mosman around 4 p.m.

The cool voice was amused. 'Oh, God no. I've got appointments myself until 6.30. Shall we say 7.45?'

Douglas A. Schirer's set-up, on the second floor in a modern office complex, bore very little resemblance to mine. These days I at least have my name and business stencilled on the door, replacing the filing card I used to have tacked there. But Schirer had gone the whole hog, with an opaque glass pane in the door carrying his name and occupation in gold lettering. Inside was a small reception area with a desk and receptionist. At my place you open the door and you've got me. The receptionist was a young, dark-haired woman who was busy at a word processor when I arrived. She seemed to be good at it and it held, or rather divided, her attention.

'I'll be with you in a moment, sir,' she said, her hands still dancing over the keys.

'Carry on.'

She did, looked satisfied, and then looked up. 'Mr Hardy?'

'That's right.'

'Go in, please. Mr Schirer is expecting you.'

I'll admit I was impressed. The young woman knew her business and there was no pretentious buzzing or announcing or offering of coffee. I knocked on the door to the left of her desk and went in.

The website photograph had flattered Schirer. He was florid and quite a few kilos overweight. If anything there was less grey in his hair and moustache than the photograph had showed, which seemed to point to vanity or concern about getting older. His handshake was a touch stronger than it needed to be.

'Glad to meet you,' he said, waving a hand at a chair and sinking back into the one behind his desk. 'Have a seat. To what do I owe the pleasure?'

The office was well appointed with serviceable furniture — filing cabinets, three solid chairs, two well-stocked bookshelves and a large-screen television with VCR. Decent carpet. Schirer's desk held a computer and assorted papers, magazines and what looked like company reports.

'It's a matter of who,' I said. 'Rodney Harkness to be precise.'

I watched closely for his reaction to the name.

'Jesus Christ. That's a blast from the past.'

Was the surprise genuine? I couldn't tell. Police detectives, some of them, get good at acting from interviewing cunning suspects and being grilled in court. Schirer could easily be one of those.

'You remember him, then?'

'Sure. Poor bugger. Bloody good actor but he got on the piss and went nuts. I heard he was put away.'

'He's out now.'

'Is he? Good on him.' He was in his shirtsleeves with his tie loosened. He seemed relaxed.

'No hard feelings, then?'

He spread his hands. 'What? About that fight? Naw, he licked me fair and square. Mind you, I was probably drunker than him.'

It was my turn to conceal surprise. I nodded my acceptance of what he said and went on as if following the same train of thought. 'Mr Harkness seems to think there could be some money for him from television commercial residuals.'

Schirer shrugged. 'I wouldn't know. I got right out of that cunt of a business.'

I felt I wasn't getting anywhere and couldn't get a good handle on Schirer. I decided to backtrack and try to catch him off guard. 'Tell me about the fight.'

'What I'll tell you is that if you're doing anything with Rod you'd better watch yourself. That guy's got a temper like you wouldn't believe and the least thing can set him off.'

'Least thing? I thought there was a fair bit of money involved.'

'Well, there might've been but, hey, I was doing all right at the time from my other irons in the fire. Anyway, it wasn't the money that set him off.'

Slippery stuff. Rod had said Schirer was on the skids. I wondered which of them was lying. 'What, then?'

'Shit, it was dumb of me I know, but we were having this . . . discussion about the nature of our contractual relationship and I got a bit annoyed and made some remark about it being only a bloody commercial, not real acting. He blew up and it was on. Another weird thing is this, I saw Rod some time after and he seemed to have forgotten all about the stoush. I said something and he acted like he didn't know what I was talking about. I wasn't surprised when I heard he was in the nuthouse.'

'Or distressed.'

He looked at his watch. 'Not really. I've been through too much myself to worry about what happens to other people. I'm sorry, I'm afraid I have to go.'

He reached into a drawer in his desk and took out a bottle of pills and a small V-shaped plastic container of liquid.

'What's that, if you don't mind me asking.'

'Medication for glaucoma, mate. I'm going fucking blind. See what I mean about not giving a shit about other people?'

PART 2

11

I had time to kill before my meeting with Dr Weir so I drove to Wesley Scott's gym in Leichhardt. I keep a pair of shorts, a T-shirt and some sneakers in the car with a threadbare towel for just such spur-of-the-moment decisions. I'd been missing sessions since starting on the Harkness case and it doesn't take long to lose the edge. I did a 15 stint on the treadmill and then went through my routines on the machines and free weights — nothing too taxing. I was back on the treadmill for a warm down when Wesley approached, interrupting my train of thought about Rodney Harkness.

'You're bludging, Cliff,' Wesley said. 'You should put another couple of plates on those machines.'

Wesley is a former champion body builder who works out himself before the mere mortals arrive. I once caught him at it, working with the full load of plates on a machine where I go less than halfway down the stack. I had the treadmill on 6 with an incline of 3.5, taking it easy.

'Don't want to bulk up,' I said.

'Huh. Haven't seen you for a bit. Busy?'

'Yes and no. I've got a babysitting job, but the

baby's proving a bit of a handful. Have you ever heard of anyone with a hair-trigger temper who explodes into violence and then seems to forget he's done it?'

Wesley shook his shaven, gleaming head and smiled. His skin is the colour of dark chocolate and his teeth are as white as a brand new golf ball.

'Roid rage?'

'No.'

'Sounds dangerous. Big guy?'

'Big enough.'

'Pent-up aggression?'

'Hard to say.'

'Bring him around. Let him work it off with the weights.'

'What if he throws one at somebody?'

'I'd keep an eye on him. He might cock it, but he wouldn't throw it.'

If a million bucks is the mean price in Mosman Dr Weir must've paid well above that because there was nothing average about her house. Given the elevation she'd have a view out over Middle Harbour and the flotilla of boats. Probably a glimpse of Balmoral Beach as well, except it was too dark now to tell. The land would have gone a bit above the quarter acre and a bit under half. It was sloping and irregularly shaped, allowing the big brick house to settle in nicely among the trees and shrubs and lawn behind high sandstone walls.

I was early but I didn't care. I parked outside behind a grey Audi, opened the gate and walked up the cement path to the house. Nothing pretentious;

triple-fronted, just twenty or so rooms with a wide verandah, bay windows, slate roof, a bit of ivy here and there. Maybe Dr Weir was an earth mother type with a dozen kids.

I approached what looked like the front door on the left side of the house and saw a door away to my right open and a man come out. He walked briskly down the path and out. The Audi started up and purred away. A well-heeled patient.

I pressed the buzzer and waited. After a minute or so a light came on overhead and I saw movement behind the peephole. The telephone voice sounded close to my shoulder.

'Mr Hardy?'

'That's right.'

The door opened and a woman stood framed against the light behind her. She was tall and slender, wearing loose dark trousers and a cream silk shirt. Medium heels. A thin gold chain. Trained observer.

'Won't you come in.'

I went in and got a closer look at her. Thirty-something, maybe more. Weir isn't an Irish name as far as I know, but she was black Irish for sure — dark eyes, blue-black hair and that dense white skin that doesn't tan, doesn't freckle, doesn't wrinkle, doesn't do anything but stay the way it is. Married name, then, but no wedding ring. 'You're a fraction early. My last patient just left.'

'I saw him. Sorry. A bad habit of mine.'

'I wouldn't say that.' She gestured for me to follow her and we went down a passage past a couple of closed doors to a big space that was part kitchen, part living room, part solarium. 'I'd say it was a habit that allowed you to catch people off guard as you have me. I was going to have a quick drink before you came. Now you're here will you join me? Just white wine.'

'Yes, thank you.'

She moved to the fridge on her medium heels and managed to make it look like a series of dance steps. She took a bottle, nudged the door shut with her knee and used the thumb and two fingers of her other hand to fork two large wine glasses off a shelf. She tilted her head and I joined her near the big window where there was a glass-topped table and some cane chairs. She flopped down into a chair keeping the bottle and glasses steady, lowered them to the table pulled the cork out with long, strong fingers. Poured.

'Cheers.'

I nodded and drank some wine. Getting on for eight o'clock and first drink of the day. Good going. She took a long pull on her glass and let out a sigh.

'Hard day?'

'They're all hard. There's so many troubled people about and so much to trouble them. I suppose you find that in your profession.'

I wasn't used to high-power professionals admitting me to their company and my instinctive reaction was to disclaim membership, but she seemed to mean it so I took it at face value. 'I wouldn't deal with nearly as many as you, doctor, and most of them probably aren't as troubled as your people. A few of them maybe more so.'

'Where would you put Rodney Harkness?'

I'd expected to be the one asking questions and this threw me slightly. Also the look on her face when she said the name. *The old Rod's got what it takes*, I thought. 'He's functioning okay,' I said. 'But he's carrying a lot of baggage.'

She nodded. 'I'm sure that's true. But what are you hoping to get from me? You must know that everything I've learned about him is strictly and utterly confidential.'

I drank some more of the good white and pondered that while I looked at her. That wasn't hard to do. She was just the other side of beautiful, with a squarish jaw and a thin upper lip that made her all the better looking. Impossible to read anything in those dark eyes and her composed body language. I remembered how she'd used his first name on the phone when her guard was down.

'Confidentiality applies pretty much the same way in my game,' I said. 'Without all the legal propping of course. What if I relax it a bit and tell you that by helping me you might save his life. He's been shot at once already.' I held up my thumb and forefinger a centimetre apart. 'Missed by about this much.'

She paused the glass on the way to her mouth and her hand shook a fraction before she got back in control. 'Jesus! Do you mean that?'

'You could take a look at my car outside. You'd find fragments of glass from the broken windshield and a bullet hole in the back seat. This happened within minutes of my driving him away from Rutherford House.'

'Did you report this to the police?'

I shook my head,

'Why not?'

'There's wheels within wheels here, doctor. We've been hired by Rod's brother and mother to investigate various aspects of his . . . circumstances. Sorry if that sounds vague. I mean, among other things, what's happened to his wife and child. I was supposed to be supportive in the early stages. Not to mince matters, to keep him away from alcohol and encourage healthy activity. It's turned into more of a protective role.'

She finished her wine and reached for the bottle. It's not everyone who finishes a glass before me. I felt virtuous, considered sitting pat, but tossed mine off as well and accepted a refill. When we were charged up again she leaned back in her chair with something of her composure restored.

'You said *we*.'

'I'm working with another detective. A woman.'

'Ah. Are you aware of Rodney Harkness's attractiveness to women?'

'I'm beginning to be.'

'Are you now? Interesting. I could read something into your response. That . . . quality of his has been the source of a great deal of his trouble, I can tell you that. I'm only confirming what you already know. I take what you say seriously, Mr Hardy, but professionally I have to be very careful. I can perhaps confirm things as I say, I can't . . . divulge, if you see the distinction.'

'I think I do. Okay. We want to find out who

was behind getting Harkness released. He doesn't know; his family doesn't know. You were recruited for your professional assessment, which was instrumental. Can you tell me by who, or is it whom?'

She smiled and I got a flash of arctic white choppers that, in the right circumstances, could be a powerful sexual signal. 'Absolutely not. I wouldn't tell you if I could and, as it happens, I don't know. Of course I asked, but the solicitors who hired me said they'd been briefed by others who wouldn't reveal who their clients were. I understand there was a civil liberties element. I suspect you'd end up gaga trying to follow that trail.'

'Didn't that concern you?'

She twisted the glass in those long fingers. 'I'll be frank. I'm writing a book about . . . certain mental disturbances. When this case was presented to me I saw it as an opportunity. I can't say any more than that.'

I leaned forward. 'You can't say what the book's about?'

'No.'

'Okay. I'll try for more confirmation. I've been told that Rodney was involved in a violent incident back before he was committed. The other person involved, who Rodney beat incidentally and he's no cream puff, said Rodney later seemed to have no memory of it at all. I've seen something similar myself — a violent rage, an excessive use of force, and apparently no recollection of it later. Does this sound familiar?'

'Yes.'

'But you recommended that he be released.'

'Mm.'

'What's wrong with this man, Dr Weir?'

She cracked a bit then. She set her glass down on the table and let her head fall forward. The dark curtain of hair swung down over her face and she spoke as if through a veil of pain.

'I can't tell you. If you find out some other way I can confirm it. It's dreadful, but I just can't tell you.'

'I think you should. At least . . . tell me something useful.'

'He's not going to overcome his problems locked away like that. Behaviourism won't work, that's for certain.'

'You've lost me.'

'I'm a Gestalt therapist, Mr Hardy. Do you know what that is?'

'No.'

She gave me a short lecture on various therapies — Gestalt, behaviourist, Jungian and Freudian — only some of which I understood. What I got out of it was that she believed in treating the whole person in his or her social, professional, recreational, intellectual, whatever, context. No dream interpretation, no Oedipal stuff. 'You've never been in therapy, Mr Hardy?'

'No.'

'No. You don't look like a man with uncertainties.'

'I wouldn't say that. Does it work?'

'Sometimes.'

'In Rodney's case?'

'I believe it would, but he resisted any suggestion that he go into therapy with me. '

'Resisted how?'

'Emphatically, defensively but emphatically.'

'I wish you could tell me more, Dr Weir.'

She gave me a look I couldn't interpret. 'So do I.'

I wanted to voice the suspicion that her reticence was partly due to personal concerns as well as professional, but I thought better of it. 'You're being enigmatic.'

She smiled, back in control again. 'Wouldn't you say that's appropriate to the human condition? It's very painful for him, but I just can't tell you.'

12

Longish day. A strong wind had got up while I was with Dr Weir. The tops of the tallest trees in her garden were whipping fiercely and I had to brace myself against the wind as I made my way to the car. I worked my way west, crossing Lane Cove and Tarban Creek to pick up the Gladesville Bridge. I had it in mind to drive to my house in Glebe to check for mail and messages, pick up some clothes and see if the roof had blown off. Halfway across the Gladesville Bridge I was almost regretting the route I'd taken; the wind hit the car like a fist and I had to fight to keep it in the lane. Two solid glasses of wine on an empty stomach could give you breathalyser trouble. That, combined with keeping a weather eye out for anyone on my tail, made for a stressful drive.

My street had a good cover of leaves and wind-blown rubbish and there were plastic bags trapped in the uprights of my sagging wrought iron fence. The roof was still on and not noticeably flapping. I checked the phone messages, the fax and the email while I heated some tomato soup and toasted some dubious-looking bread.

I resisted the impulse to have a drink but packed the half full Scotch bottle into an overnight bag with a couple of shirts, some underwear and socks. I wolfed the food down and rang the Bondi flat. I got my own voice on the answering machine but no pick up.

I made some coffee and rang again with the same result. *Where the hell are you?* I thought. As I drank the coffee I thought back over the events of the day. Doug Schirer was apparently out of the picture as an antagonist and certainly as a shooter. After my talk with the psychiatrist I felt I hardly knew Rodney St John Harkness at all. What was his deep, dark secret? For no good reason what he'd said after the shooting came back to me. *Haven't you got a gun?* I took my Smith & Wesson .38 in its holster out of the locked drawer and stuffed it into the overnight bag. The intrepid detective, completely in the dark but ready for anything.

In Bondi I drove around the block a few times for security reasons and on the lookout for Glen's Pajero. No sign. The wind was roaring and the night had an uncertain, dangerous feel as if unexpected things might happen. It was an unusual atmosphere for Bondi, a place that has always seemed to me to give off an aura of optimism. I went up to the flat and knocked before I let myself in. No response.

I prowled through the rooms, noting the signs of a great deal of coffee being drunk and time spent at the computer. There were Post-its stuck to the monitor as reminders of functions to perform.

I'd straightened the bed I'd slept in before I left. So far I hadn't seen Rod do anything to his bed but get in and out of it. Now it was neatly made. I went into the room I was using and dropped my bag. A Post-it was on the bed, dead centre.

Cliff— Glen and I have taken some time out. We'll be in touch. Rod.

I took out the Scotch, went to the kitchen and poured a hefty slug. Not much water. I sat down with the drink, thinking harsh thoughts of both of them. *Bloody alcoholics. You can't expect them to behave properly.* I worked on the drink and other ideas began to seep in. There was something worrying about two recovering alcoholics being on the loose together. Would they reinforce each other's sobriety or fall off the wagon together? If so, how hard? Did whoever was out to get Rod have a line on Glen? Probably not, but you never knew. He knew when Rod was getting out and that knowledge wasn't supposed to be shared by any except the Harknesses, Glen and me, and some people at Rutherford House. The security didn't feel watertight.

The Scotch soothed me and I began to feel less angry and more worried. Rodney Harkness was an unknown quantity harbouring some dark, painful secret. I'd seen his violent outbursts and apparent lack of remorse or responsibility afterwards. Glen was tough and resourceful but Rod had got under her guard very quickly and she was vulnerable. Was she safe with him?

I had a refill and went out onto the balcony to

drink it and see how the weather was shaping. The wind was howling now; TV antennas and satellite dishes were wobbling and tall trees were thrashing. I finished the drink and realised that the amount of Scotch I'd taken in had hit me hard and I was half-drunk. *Where the fuck are you?* I felt like shouting it into the wind. Tomorrow I'd have to think more clearly about it — consider Glen's favourite places — the Blue Mountains, the Southern Highlands — find out if Rod had any in his former life. Surfing spots most likely. Byron Bay for its point break?

I went back inside and rang Glen's mobile number. I got the recorded message that the phone was out of range or had been switched off. Wandering from room to room, something about the ultra modern, pastel-shaded computer drew me to it. I read the blizzard of Post-its. Glen had set him up with a server for email and the Internet. I put the dregs of my drink down on the desk, settled into the chair and turned the computer on. It took me a while with the unfamiliar functions but I remembered how to get onto my server's mail centre and access my own email. I tapped out a message for Glen. I knew she took a notebook with her everywhere and checked for messages frequently. I deleted the first angry sentence and the next that I mistyped badly because I was half-drunk as well as angry. I ended up with:

Glen — This is unwise. There's a lot you don't know and need to know. Get in touch as soon as you see this and tell me where you are.

No sign of jealousy there, surely. No alarmism. Just professional concern with a touch of superior knowledge to engage her curiosity. I looked at the message for a long time, knowing that it was nothing like what I really wanted to say. How could this dysfunctional loser of an actor, this overgrown private schoolboy with his perfect teeth and tight abdominals, turn intelligent women to mush? I clicked on Send harder than I needed to, waited for the message to vanish, and turned the computer off. I realised at that moment that I wasn't thinking about Rodney or Glen but about Dr Jerry Weir with her curtain of dark hair and her dancer's grace.

I poured some more whisky, rang Glen's home number and left the same message on her answering machine, word for word. I felt lonely and self-pitying in the flat and turned on the radio for company. It was tuned to a country music station. Glen again. Her favourite music. Not mine. With Rod, who knew what he liked apart from Elvis? I drowned the Scotch in water and hunted around for the pain-killers I'd need sometime between now and the morning. No luck. I heard:

There's a pain in my heart
Like a lightning bolt,
I'm a little bit lonesome
It's all your fault.

'Right,' I said to the print of a watercolour of nowhere in particular on the wall, and raised my glass. 'That's right.' But I knew in *my* heart that it was never true.

13

I slept long and deeply, undisturbed by dreams or by the wild night. I was reasonably clear-headed and after a couple of cups of coffee and a shower I was alert enough to take note of a few things like Rod's missing toilet articles, clothes and overnight bag. The surfboard was gone as well and I could imagine it riding high on the roof rack of Glen's Pajero. My first thought was, *To hell with them*, but I wasn't comfortable with it and out of professional pride I began to think about ways of finding them. The surfboard was a lead. Maybe Rod had favourite beaches. The snag with that was the only person I had to ask was his brother and I didn't want to let him know that his private eye had flown the coop with the client.

Still mulling it over I punched in the code to check my phone messages at the office. There were three, two of which didn't matter but the third did. The voice was unfamiliar: 'Mr Hardy, this is Brett Hughes. Frank Parker spoke to you about me to do with Rodney Harkness. I'm keen to talk to you. I believe you have my number. Give me a ring.'

I'd barely given the ex-policeman a thought since Frank had told me about him but it had been at the back of my mind to contact him to see if he could give me anything I could take to Dr Weir. I didn't like shelving the question of the runaway love birds, but Hughes' message had a certain urgency. I dug out my notebook, looked up the scribbled note and rang him. He lived in Lakemba and we arranged to meet at a coffee shop in Haldon Street in an hour.

I shaved, put on a clean shirt and went out to the car. Then I cursed myself and went back into the flat to check whether Glen had sent a reply to my email. Nothing. The wind had died down, leaving a clear sky and clean air that quickly became a memory as I went west and battled against heavy traffic going in several directions. Lakemba, with its concentration of Muslim and Asian migrants, has been an unquiet place for some time and more so since the attack on New York and Washington. According to newspaper reports, the initial unthinking racist reaction has died down but it simmers.

Early as always, I parked a couple of blocks from the number on the street Hughes had given me to kill some time and look the place over. I hadn't been there in quite a while and in this business it pays to stay abreast of the changes. There were plenty — Arabic and Korean contended for dominance on the shopfronts and hoardings and beards and veils were prominent on the street. I couldn't help liking it — the change from the blandness of the eastern suburbs in my youth and the uniformity that still prevails in the privileged parts of Sydney. But I could feel the pressure: some of the bearded men were unfashionably fat but prosperous-looking, and a good many of the Anglo–Celtic youths were thin and poor and with many of the thin, light-boned Asians it was hard to tell.

The coffee shop had an outside pavement area with tables and shade umbrellas. I told them inside that I was waiting for a friend and that I'd order when he arrived.

The woman behind the counter wore an abbreviated version of the female Arab costume but she said 'No problem' like a true Aussie. I took a seat and watched the passing parade. I was considering trying to phone Glen's house and the Bondi flat when a wheelchair rolled up beside me. The occupant was a man a good deal younger than me with wide shoulders and a deep chest. His face was lean and hard. He looked as if he could throw a discus or put the shot out of sight, but he was anchored to the chair. He stuck out a big hand.

'Mr Hardy? Frank described you. I'm Brett Hughes.' We shook hands and he wheeled himself in close to the table. I ordered two coffees and, remembering that I hadn't eaten anything that morning, a toasted sandwich. He didn't want to eat.

'Strict diet,' he said. 'Big danger of this kind of life is getting fat. I swim and work out but nothing beats normal movement.'

I nodded. 'Frank said you took a bullet.'

'Two actually. Zapped my spine. Did he tell you I got the guy who shot me?'

'No.'

'He's dead. I'm not. I win.' His grin took the bitterness out of it and I admired him. The coffee and the sandwich arrived and we went through the ritual of drinking before talking. I started eating because I figured he wanted to have first say.

'I was interested when Frank Parker phoned me. I'd always been curious about that Harkness business. I arrested him, you knew that.'

I nodded, said nothing.

'Yeah, he'd beaten the living shit out of this guy in a pub. I just happened to be there. Wasn't on duty. I was super fit in those days and I'll tell you it took me all my time to get him under control. When we got to the lockup he broke free and took to one of the officers there. Tough bloke but Harkness put him in the hospital, multiple fractures. Again, it took three of us to subdue him.'

I finished the sandwich and the coffee. 'Most of this is new to me,' I said. 'I mean the detail. But I had the gist. When you say you were curious about him . . .'

'Yeah, well, a couple of the blokes at the station wanted me to go in and give him a good kicking, you know? I might've too, I was pretty angry. I went into the cell and he was babbling. Drunk, but not that drunk by now, not after everything that'd gone on over an hour and a bit.'

'Let me guess,' I said. 'He seemed to have forgotten all about it. As if it'd never happened.'

Hughes looked surprised. 'That's right. I kind of got him to stop talking and tried to tell him what an arsehole he was and he didn't know what I was talking about. He went right on spewing out this stuff.'

'What stuff?'

'He was saying he'd killed his wife and kid. Not sort of, really. Actually killed them.'

'He was pissed.'

'Like I say, not *that* pissed. Sounded like he meant it.'

'And you reported this?'

'No.' He swivelled and looked along the street at the multicultural parade as if he was gazing backward in time to when he had full control of his body. 'I shouldn't, but I'm going to have another coffee. Coffee's real bad shit, you know. You can't drink it when you go on a homeopathic course. It's toxic as hell. You have to clear it out of your system first up.'

'That right?' I signalled for the waitress and ordered two more long blacks. When they came he stirred in two spills of sugar, breaking all the rules. 'I envy you, man. When we finish here you're going to jump in your car and go chasing after what comes next. Right?'

'I wouldn't say jump, but yeah, that's more or less right. Why didn't you report what Harkness said, Brett?'

'I thought about it and I was going to but then his brother and solicitor arrived and I found out he was an actor and that changed my mind. See, what he'd been babbling was like in two voices. He'd say something in one voice, and then something else in another quite different voice. Changing from one to the other real quick. When they told me he was a TV actor I figured he was remembering some old script or something. Sounded just like some of that crap. Then I heard that he was being taken out of circulation and I let it go.'

At least now I had something to take to Jerry Weir, but Hughes had more to say. 'I wanted to tell you this when Frank Parker told me that you were minding Harkness and that someone had taken a shot at him.'

'Yes?'

'Thinking back I don't reckon he was quoting from a script. I reckon he was confessing to killing his wife and kid. And it's likely there's someone out there who wants him for that, wouldn't you say?'

14

Brett Hughes finished his coffee and began playing with the paper napkin, folding it into smaller and smaller squares. 'I've given you a problem, have I?' he said. 'I was sort of thinking I might be helpful. Talking like this, getting that call from Parker. Felt like old times. I miss the job. Still miss it like hell after all these years.'

Right then I was thinking that I could do without my job very easily. It was getting complicated the way it can, with new information piling in on the old and contradicting it or calling it into serious question. I shook my head to make him feel better. 'No, mate. It's useful information, I just don't quite know how to make use of it. The thing is, this woman I'm working with has taken off with Harkness. So it's a question of how dangerous he is.'

He unfolded the napkin. 'Very, I'd say. Sorry.'

'The psychiatrist who recommended his release says he isn't.'

'Did he know about the confession? That's how you could see it now, I have to say.'

'She. Yeah, I suspect she did. Wouldn't talk to me about it though.'

Hughes shrugged his massive shoulders. 'That's another funny thing now I come to remember. There was this rookie detective around when we were dealing with Harkness. Mary something. She was with the sergeant when they took him some coffee after he'd calmed down. I was a bit keen on her. We all were . . .' He broke off and looked as if he might go back to napkin folding but he didn't. 'Anyway, I had a word with her afterwards and she reckoned Harkness was the biggest spunk she'd seen in years. And she was a good-looker. From the way she talked about him I reckon he could've had her on her back in no time flat.'

'Yeah, he's still like that, it seems. But that raises a point. Did you talk to anyone at the station about what Harkness had said about killing his wife and kid?'

Hughes lifted one of his hands and stroked the side of his face. I could see the calluses at the base of the fingers where the mitts hadn't quite protected his hands from the weights bars. 'Jeez, now you're asking. It's a long time ago and not that long before all this shit happened.' He slammed his hands down on his thighs. 'I remember that I was thinking about reporting it like I said until the acting came up. So I would've been thinking about how to write it up. Don't think I talked to anyone, but shit, I just can't remember.'

'Do you remember exactly who was in the station at the time?'

He shook his head. 'Not right off. I could probably work it out, but. Oh, I get it. You're thinking about who'd know that he said he killed them. But you're talking about police officers.'

'There's cops and cops,' I said. 'No civilians there? Clerks? Drunks?'

'Don't think so, but I'd need peace and quiet to think about it.'

I gave him a card with my contact details on it. 'If you come up with anything I'd be very grateful if you'd get in touch. And thanks for this.'

He grinned. 'Too easy, and you're paying for the coffees, right?'

I put money on the table. We shook hands again and it became one of those awkward moments between the able-bodied and the handicapped. He pushed off and I said, 'Can I . . . help you on your way?'

'No, mate. I can drive myself. I've got a car all hooked up. I'll be right. Just stay right where you are if you don't mind.'

I watched him swivel the wheelchair and scoot away along the pavement. He stopped at a white Honda Civic and with a bit of lifting and shoving manoeuvred himself into the driver's seat, and for that moment my problems didn't seem so big at all.

'Time out' — what does that mean? How long? I had no idea. I tossed up whether to try to talk to Dr Weir and learn more about Rodney Harkness's 'confession' in the hope that it might give me some lead, or to keep after Glen by phone and email. Neither approach seemed promising. I found myself driving back to Bondi with no particular plan in mind, just a vague hope that the Pajero might be there and that 'time out' meant twenty-four hours. No such luck.

I parked in the allotted carport for the flat and went up the stairs. The door was standing open with splintering around the lock. I felt my pulse increase and the adrenalin kick in. My gun was in my bag under the bed and I had to hope whoever had broken in hadn't found it. I looked along the concrete walkway for a weapon and the only thing in sight was a kid's skateboard lying wheels up outside a flat further along. Better than nothing. I scuttled along and grabbed it.

I went in low and fast, shouting and whacking anything in sight with the skateboard. He came out of Rod's bedroom carrying the iMac. A big guy. Young. He dropped the computer and yelled when he saw me. The adrenalin-pumped momentum drove me forward and I rammed hard at his groin with the skateboard. I missed, caught him on the thigh and didn't hurt him much. He lashed out and got me on the side of the head. I reeled back and he came on, still yelling, scared and angry. Dangerous as hell. I was slightly dazed but I still had the skateboard. I swung it backhand against his left knee and caught it just right so that it collapsed inwards. He went down but he wasn't finished. I moved in and he just missed with a lashing kick. I slammed the side of the skateboard against his ear and the wheels bit into the back of his head and that was enough for him. He flopped back on the carpet, panting and bleeding.

I straddled him, holding the board hard under his jaw, forcing his head back. 'Now just who the hell are you?'

'What . . . what d'you mean? I just come along and seen the door busted, and . . .'

I'd practically been cutting off his wind but now I eased back. 'You didn't break in?'

'No, man. I swear. I just . . .'

'Okay, okay. When was this? How long've you been here?'

'No time. I seen the computer and grabbed it. Then you come in. Fuck, I was scared.'

'You should be. Break and enter, theft, assault. Serious charges.'

'Look. I told you. I never broke in.'

'Hard to prove. The Bondi cops don't like thieving pricks like you.'

The look in his eyes told me that he was in complete agreement. For a second he thought about giving it another go but I increased the pressure on his jaw and his head fell back again. The carpet was a bloody mess by now and he was white-faced under his stubble and shaking. He smelled bad.

'You a user?'

He sniffed and nodded.

'Had your eye on this place did you?'

'Yeah, seen the fuckin' Pajero and the sheilah . . . you know. Looked like she had a bit.'

I wasn't convinced, not with everything that was going on. Had someone employed him to look for something, maybe to get the computer? 'I think we need the cops,' I said.

'Jesus, man, no. Don't do that. I couldn't take it.

Look, I told you, I didn't break in and you haven't lost nothing.'

'Why'd you take the computer?'

'To get money for a fix. Why'd you fuckin' think?'

In a strange way the belligerence and mood swing lent him credibility. It seemed unlikely that Rod's pursuer, who'd played some pretty cunning tricks, would resort to a loser like this as an assistant. I took one hand away, reached for my wallet and showed him my licence. 'I'm a private investigator and you've got yourself into something you don't want to know about. If you tell me everything you've seen here, and I mean *everything*, I'll think about letting you go. Otherwise it's the cops, and it still will be if you bullshit me.'

'Sure. Sure thing.'

'What's your name?'

'Craig, Craig Griffiths.'

'Okay, Craig. Where d'you live?'

'Shit, man, why d'you want to know?'

'Two reasons — so I can find you if I need to and so I can check on what you say if I have to.'

He gave me an address that might or might not have been true. It's always wise to give someone you're questioning an easy one first up and it helps to gauge truthfulness. Craig seemed keen to help and I wondered if perhaps I'd encountered him on his second visit and he already had a few things from the flat tucked away.

'When did you start watching the flat?'

'When I first seen the Pajero, like yesterday morning.'

'Kept an eye on it ever since?'

'Sort of, yeah.'

'Anyone else watching?'

'How d'you mean?'

'Like I say. Was there anyone else showing an interest in the place?'

I could tell by the flicker in his eyes that he was considering lying. I put the pressure back on his throat. 'Don't even think about it, mate. Doesn't matter how scary he was, I can be worse.'

'There was this bloke today, yeah.'

'The one who broke in?'

He nodded and hurt himself. 'Shit! Yeah.'

'Description.'

'Big guy, big as me. Fit like.'

'More. Hair, clothes, age.'

'Shit, not much hair, sort of baldie with it clipped close. Dark suit. Dunno about how old — forty, fifty.'

'Come on.'

'Younger than you.'

'A lot of people are younger than me, but we'll let that go. Vehicle?'

'Camry. New.'

'Colour?'

'Red.'

'Registration?'

'Dunno.'

'Tell me what happened, Craig, and get it right.'

Craig wasn't much of a storyteller, but with plenty of prompting I got a disjointed but detailed account of how the man in the Camry had pulled up outside the building, made a call on his mobile, waited, gone up to the flat and returned to his car. He'd opened the boot and taken out a tyre iron. Craig had positioned himself on the level below and heard the door splinter. He said the intruder had been inside for perhaps ten minutes. After he'd left Craig had made his own entry and I'd surprised him almost immediately.

I'd let him sit up by this time but I positioned myself between him and the doorway and kept the skateboard handy. 'For a second there I thought this fucker had come back.'

'I'm not bald, Craig, and I'm not wearing a suit.'

'Didn't mean that, man. I meant the kind of bloke he was.'

'I don't get it.'

Craig wasn't the brightest and he fumbled for words to express his meaning. After a few moments of struggle he brushed his index finger against his upper lip. 'Shit, I forgot to say he had this fuckin' moustache. He looked like a cop. That's what I meant when I reckoned he was like you, not looked like, *like*, see?'

I saw. All in all it was a pretty good description although a worrying one. Craig rubbed at his knee and throat and looked as if he was longing to be somewhere else.

'Stand up,' I said. 'See if you can walk.'

He levered himself up against the wall behind him and stood unsteadily. He took a couple of limping steps forward and grabbed at the edge of the table.

'Those stairs are going to be a problem.'

'I can do it, man.'

I nodded. 'You saw the bloke who left with the woman yesterday.'

He touched his upper lip. 'Yeah, big bloke with the Elvis T-shirt.'

'That's him. He owns the computer. If it's buggered I don't think you'd want to meet him. He might be back any minute so I think you'd better piss off.'

He limped towards the door and stopped in the door frame, still rubbing at the skin under his jaw.

'Something?' I said.

'You're full of it if you reckon that bloke's goin' be back soon.'

'How's that?'

'They bought petrol at the station down the street. Looked like a full tank. I was watching. Took a while. They're long gone.'

I jerked my head at him to leave and then had a thought. 'Who was driving?'

'Him.'

Craig limped away leaving me very worried. Somebody knew where Rodney Harkness had been holing up and, depending on what he might've found in the flat, who with. As for Rod and Glen with their full tank in the Pajero and the surfboard on top, Glen didn't as a rule let anyone drive her precious car, and the man driving it didn't have a licence and hadn't driven for seven years.

15

I replaced the computer, plugged it in and switched it on. The smiling Macintosh face came up and the desktop screen appeared and it seemed to have survived the fall. I checked my email in the hope that Glen had responded to my message but she hadn't. I checked my phone messages again with the same result. I made some coffee, considered spiking it with the remainder of the whisky and decided against. I prowled around the flat to see if anything was missing. My gun was where it should be. A relief.

Junkies these days mostly steal money because you can't get anything much for second-hand electronic equipment and the hock shops are more tightly regulated than they used to be. Maybe Craig was hoping to acquire some new skills by pinching the iMac. The TV and VCR and the microwave and the transistor radio were all present and correct. There hadn't been any money lying around that I recalled. I went into each room a couple of times with the vague feeling that something *was* missing, but I couldn't pin down what it was.

The clothes Rod had left and the few in my room would've told the intruder that Harkness had a minder, but if he was the same one who'd fired the shots he'd have known that already. I couldn't see that there was any sign of Glen's presence — no stockings in the bathroom, no lipstick stains on a cup or a glass. Then it came to me. I'd put the Post-it Rod had left on the bedside table in my room and it had gone.

So he had a name and if he really was a cop as Craig had suspected he'd have ways and means. Glen could be a man's name but there was no comfort in that thought. This guy, I suspected, knew Harkness well, knew he was straight and that he was off in the wild blue yonder with a woman named Glen. Put like that it didn't sound like much of a lead. I realised that the intruder and I were in much the same boat — urgently looking for two people on the basis of very slender information,

I swore and kicked at the skateboard lying on the living room floor. It skidded across the carpet and crashed into the wall and made me feel foolish. I picked it up and went through the broken door with it in my hand intending to put it back where I'd found it. I was standing there, with the child's toy dangling from my hand, when I heard footsteps coming up the stairs and Warren St John Harkness in all his pinstriped glory came into view.

He stopped a metre away, removed his sunglasses and stared at me and the splintered door. 'What in the name of God are you doing?'

Good question, I thought. I bent, skidded the skateboard along the concrete walkway, and had the satisfaction of seeing it stop near enough to where I'd found it. 'You'd better come in, Mr Harkness. We've got a few things to talk about.'

There was no point in holding anything back so I gave it to him, chapter and verse. It was a lot to take in all at once but lawyers are used to processing information and he stayed quiet until I'd finished, mentally filing everything I said. I put the best spin on it I could, letting him know that his holding back information on his brother's difficulties and character hadn't helped. From the way he took it he seemed to be registering it as valid, at least in part. But he wasn't going on the back foot.

'I don't think I've ever heard of such incompetence.'

I let that pass. 'What brought you here today, Mr Harkness?'

'I'd heard nothing from Ms Withers for two days. She was supposed to make daily reports.'

'That's news to me. Why didn't you tell us about Rodney's belief that he killed his wife and child?'

'It was a delusion.'

'That doesn't answer the question.'

'And I don't intend to.'

'Why did you hire a female investigator when you knew about Rodney's capacity to charm women?'

'Don't be ridiculous. He's almost forty, he . . .'

'He can still do it.'

'I'm sorry to hear it. It was one of the sources of his trouble.'

We were standing a metre apart in the living room, which was littered with things I'd knocked down with the skateboard as I launched my attack — books, a broken chair, coffee mugs. There was a dark patch on the carpet where Craig had bled.

'What happened here?' Harkness said.

'It doesn't matter. Why don't you sit down. Something's just struck me and I want to try it out on you.'

He glanced at his gold watch. 'I haven't got much time.'

'Won't take long.'

He pulled a chair out from the living room table and sat as if it had a nail sticking up. I perched on the edge of the table.

'I've got a feeling that you hired a female investigator and an attractive one because you knew your brother would . . . form an attachment, shall we say?'

'Why would we do that?'

I registered the 'we' but didn't let it distract me. 'I think you also knew that Glen Withers has a drinking problem. Rodney has a reputation for violence. That's a volatile mix. I suspect you hoped to find out whether Rodney really did kill his wife and child and Glen would act as . . . what's it called — the Judas goat.'

'That's fanciful.'

'I was insurance that things wouldn't go too far.'

He stroked his clean-shaven jowls. 'A long bow, Hardy.'

'It makes sense. If you got solid indications that Rodney did kill them you've removed an inheritance complication. Rodney's controllable, you've demonstrated that; his daughter's a very loose end. I'd be interested in the provisions of your father's will.'

That reminded me of Frank's remark about there being something dodgy about old Harkness's death, but I thought I'd said enough for the moment.

Harkness looked at me as if I was an alien creature. My hair was a mess, I had blood on my shirt and my pants were through at the knees from when I'd straddled Craig. He wasn't used to dealing with roughnecks and it worried him.

'Pure speculation,' he said, but without much conviction.

I shook my head. 'Only partly. The question is, where do we go from here? We've got two very vulnerable people on the loose and a very dangerous person out after one of them who probably doesn't give a shit what happens to the other one. So tell me — have you got any idea who might want to kill Rodney? I'm assuming for the moment it isn't you or your mother.'

'That's offensive.'

'So is a lot of your behaviour. Glen Withers is my friend. I don't want to see her come to harm on account of your shitty manipulations.'

There was a long pause while he worked his way past outrage through calculation to compromise. 'I have no idea who this person might be. No idea at all. Hardy, I think we'd better call a truce.'

It took a while to get there. We thrashed it out a bit, both trying to gain the advantage. He claimed that he could sack Glen for incompetence and I countered with my accusations about his motives. He agreed that the important thing was to find Glen and Rodney and then decide what to do next. Privately, I thought he exhibited some unconcern about his brother's safety, not to mention Glen's, but I didn't raise it. If I was going to find the pair I'd need funds and he was the source. I still had a few questions for him though.

'They took the surfboard you bought him,' I said. 'Did Rodney have any favourite surfing spots?'

He shrugged and got off the chair. 'Don't ask me. I never took any interest in Rodney's absurd sporting pursuits. The only games I ever played with him were cards — five hundred, poker and the like — and he cheated.'

'Glen's a red-hot card player. If he tries that on her she'll roast him alive.'

He moved towards the door, uninterested, 'Really?'

'One more thing. I suppose you provided Glen with a list of his friends. Maybe there's someone he'd go to at a time like this.'

He turned back to me. 'I did no such thing. As far as I know, Rodney had no friends. I have to go.'

He went. If he'd stayed I'd have been tempted to ask him if *he* had any friends. I doubted it. What a family.

What did Gough Whitlam call Billy McMahon? 'Tiberius with a telephone'? I always liked that. I spent the next few hours phoning everyone I could think of who had any substantial connection with Glen, but I came up empty. I had to hope that she wouldn't want to miss her AA meetings but I didn't know where or when they were held. The only contact I had for Rod was his last agent, Barney Nugent.

He sounded wary. 'Rod? Yes, I was his agent.'

'I don't suppose he's been in touch with you recently?'

'You don't suppose right. What's this about? If Rod owes you money forget it, he's in the loony bin.'

'He's out, Mr Nugent, and he doesn't owe me money. In fact, I was wondering if you owed him any.'

His laugh was genuine and angry. 'Get off! What gave you that idea?'

I filled him in a bit then, enough to convince him that I was concerned about Rod and was looking for him. I mentioned the residuals payments and got the harsh, barking laugh again.

'Those residuals ran out years ago and they were on a reducing scale.'

'Still, there was money . . .'

'Listen, I gave Rod so many advances he'd have to be like Russell Crowe to pay it back. He's well in the red with me.'

'What did he spend the money on?'

'What they all spend it on — coke, booze, women.'

My next phone call was to Dr Jerry Weir.

16

'Dr Weir, this is Cliff Hardy. I've learned something about Rodney Harkness I want you to confirm, if you will.'

'Not something to discuss on the telephone. You'd better come over here.'

She suggested a time a good deal earlier than previously. That and her willingness to see me surprised me, but I put it down to her interest in Rodney. I cleaned myself up and changed my clothes. The shirt would need dry cleaning; the drill pants were a write-off. Jeans now and a cream linen shirt. Shouldn't be any blood about in Mosman. I had a swelling and an abrasion where Craig had kicked me, which would make the spot tender for a couple of days and make shaving difficult. I heated the rest of the coffee in the microwave and ate some biscuits with tinned tuna and bread and butter cucumbers. Classy, except that I ate standing up at the sink, worrying.

I tidied up the living room but left the blood patch alone. Salt on red wine, I knew that, but I could never remember whether it was good or bad on blood. Salt and blood — it sounded right but I wasn't sure. *What the hell,* I thought, *Warren's up for the bond on the flat.* The same went for the damaged door. I pulled it closed and tapped some of the splintered wood back into place and it didn't look too bad. I doubted that Craig would make another try for the iMac. This time, though, I took the .38 with me.

The traffic was sluggish and I wasn't feeling super sharp myself. I wondered if the cop look-alike who'd broken into the flat had kept a watching brief on it and was on my tail. I almost wished he was and I flicked my eyes to all three rear-vision mirrors as I went but there was no sign of a red Camry or any other interested vehicle. It was a little after five o'clock when I got to Dr Weir's house, well before my self-imposed, often violated, drinking hour, but I badly needed one. Maybe Dr Weir was feeling the same.

The street was quiet with no sign of a client's car as on my previous visit. I went up to the house in the better light more able to take in its features. What they added up to was good taste and a lot of money. I toyed with the idea of going to the client's entrance but resisted. I realised that I was in a strange mood. The Harkness case had turned out to have bends and curves in it that were hard to negotiate. Finding Glen and Rod were the priorities now, but doing that wouldn't put us a centimetre closer to the original terms of the investigation. At least in talking to Jerry Weir I was dealing with the up-front and the underlying problems. I was rehearsing what I had to say in my head as I pressed the buzzer. I was a minute or two early again.

This time the door opened almost immediately. She'd been waiting. She wore a red silk shirt tucked into loose white trousers with low-heeled sandals. Her blue-black hair gleamed and her dark eyes looked huge against her pearly complexion. I'm sure I stared and maybe just fell short of gaping.

'Come in, Mr Hardy. God, what happened to your face?'

'A kick,' I said. 'It doesn't feel as bad as it looks.'

She tilted her head to one side and I went in. 'I wouldn't say it looks bad.'

We went through to the same living space as before and she had that same grace of movement that made you want to watch her and see what she'd do next. She stopped and leaned against the fridge with one long arm extended.

'A drink?'

'I was hoping you'd offer.'

She did her glass spearing trick again but this time the bottle had to be opened. She did that with a waiter's friend, expertly applied. She poured an inch into a glass and tossed it off. She grinned. 'Just making sure it's okay.'

'Good idea. I do that, too.'

She filled the big glasses and we took our seats across from each other with the low table in between. She took a hefty belt of the wine and sighed.

'I won't ask if it's been a hard day,' I said. 'You reckon they all are.'

'That's right, but I didn't get kicked in the head, at least. I felt like kicking a few though.'

That surprised me, didn't sound therapist-like but I could imagine the feeling. I drank some wine and felt almost instantly better the way you do, although the alcohol hasn't had time to get into the bloodstream. The taste promises that it will and promises are soothing in themselves right up until they're broken. She put her glass down and stretched. Her breasts rose under the shirt and I could see that her stomach was flat. I heard a few joints creak though; she was over forty at a guess, but not as far over as me.

'Forty-three,' she said. 'You were guessing my age.'

'Jesus.'

'Did you get it right?'

I nodded. 'Close enough.'

'What about you?'

I told her, shaving a year.

'Mm, you've lived 'em, but your genes are serving you well I'd say. So . . . tell me what you think you know.'

'Rodney Harkness believes, or did believe, at least on some level, that he killed his wife and child.'

She picked up her glass, had a drink and put it down again. She placed her palms together and rubbed them like someone trying to start a fire with friction. 'You put it well. Level's a good word for what goes on in Rodney's head. Levels, or layers perhaps. His fantasies and realities and drives and needs all overlie each other and interlap. A very interesting case.'

'But he was more than just a case to you.'

'Yes and no. Sex was terribly important to him. It is to me as well. God knows, it's important to everyone. You agree?'

'Sure.'

'I wanted to have sex with him because I was attracted, but also to see how he behaved under those pressures and stimuli.'

'Aren't there professional rules about that?'

She laughed, flashing those teeth. 'What percentage of therapists fuck their patients, d'you think? All things being equal. Did you see *The Prince of Tides*?'

'Yeah, but . . .'

She waved her long, pale hand. 'Forget it. So where are we? Yes, Rodney's got that shadow in his mind.'

'You don't think he did it?'

'No. But there's something else just as bad. Oh, I'm sure he believed that he did it. As you say, on one level.'

'You've lost me.'

'Never mind. What's been happening? Who kicked you?'

The wine worked on me and I suppose her experience at extracting stories. I told her just about everything I knew. She listened intently, only breaking off to get us more wine. When I finished she came and sat on the edge of the table with her knees almost touching mine. 'I doubt she's in danger,' she said. 'Not from Rodney. But this other person . . .'

'Has to think that Rodney is responsible and

wants to make him pay for it.'

'Yes. I suppose so. Do you have any idea who that might be?'

'No. That's the frustrating thing. You'd have to assume it's someone connected to the wife and I haven't got any leads on that. Glen's the one with the information on her.'

'So you have to find her for that reason as well. You've got a job on your hands, Mr Hardy.'

She was very close now. I could smell her perfume and the wine on her breath. I felt an aching need to touch her and had begun to move my hand to hers when I felt her cool palm against my battered face. In a couple of quick head adjustments we were kissing and our mouths were locked together and opening and our tongues were probing and her thin upper lip was hard against mine, pressing against my teeth. We broke for breath and kissed again more slowly and expertly, and then we both stood and our bodies closed hard together, chest to knee.

I wrapped my arms around her and her mouth came up close to my ear on the undamaged side. 'I liked the look of you the first time,' she said. 'You're the way you want to be, aren't you?'

With my ex-wife Cyn and other women that had been an accusation; now, with her, it was a plus.

'Yes.'

'That's good. That's so good. I don't see much of that. Come with me, Cliff.'

Her bedroom was spartan — polished floor, low queen-size bed, dark cotton sheets, bedside chests, wooden slat blinds. She turned on a bedside light and pressed herself up against me. No words. We undressed each other and our hands ran over each other. She was lithe and muscular, just a bit soft in the places the years most affect. When I was ready she stepped away, took a condom packet from the bedside table, selected one and rolled it onto me with the proficiency of someone who knew what she was doing. I let her set the pace as we lay on the bed kissing and stroking. In the dim light her body was a wonderful array of planes and shadows and I explored it with the sort of excitement and confidence I hadn't felt for a long time.

'Now,' she said. 'Come into me now.'

I did and our bodies locked together and drew apart and found a rhythm that pleased us both and we stayed with it. Then she rolled to the side, pulling me with her, and she gasped and I could feel her muscles contracting and gripping and she came in a long, vibrant spasm that seemed to draw me deeper as I slithered in a sweat slick half on top of her. Then I was moaning something into her rose-smelling hair as I came.

'Ah, no,' she said as we separated and I stayed as close as I could with one hand cradling her head and the other on her hip. Her hair was damp from sweat and her skin was moist. She had one hand in the greying hair on my chest and the other somewhere else.

'Good?' she said.

'Very good, very, very good.'

'Mm. Not much else to say, is there?'

'Not about the sex. Except . . .'

'What?'

'I hope it's not the only time.'

'We'll see.' She nestled close and sniffed at me. 'You don't smoke, do you?'

'No.'

'I bet you like a drink after, though, right?'

'It's been known.'

'I'll have first shower then I'll make us something to eat and we can finish the bottle and continue our talk. I had the feeling you were going to ask me a question before we started rutting.'

She eased herself away from me and slid gracefully from the bed. She picked up her clothes and hung them on the handles of the built-in wardrobes, another thing I do myself. I enjoyed watching her move.

'I'm having trouble remembering what the questions were,' I said. 'But I guess they'll come back.'

She took a white silk dressing-gown from the back of the door and slopped into it. 'Bathroom's on the right down the passage. Give me a couple of minutes. Don't snoop.'

She'd read me right. Left alone in someone's private spaces I find snooping hard to resist. I lay back on the bed looking up at the ceiling rose as the intense pleasure of the encounter slowly ebbed away. I was thinking how strange it was that I was here having sex with the woman who'd been instrumental in getting Rodney Harkness released, while he was off no doubt doing the same thing with my professional partner. The thought of how Lady Rachel and Warren St John would react to this made me smile and she caught me at it. She came back into the room, rubbing with a towel at her wet hair and began to put her clothes on.

'Pleased with yourself?'

I explained quickly what had made me smile and she gathered up my shirt and pants and tossed them to me. 'I always thought they sounded like a pair of shits,' she said.

I showered and dressed and went back to the living room where she'd laid out some dips, cheeses, olives, tomatoes and hot focaccia bread. The wine glasses were full and she was loading up a coffee pot.

'Help yourself. Nothing fancy.'

I sat on the two-person cane couch hoping she'd join me and she did. We drank our wine and picked at the food and the feeling of her next to me, touching as we ate and drank, was better than food and drink.

'Okay,' she said. 'I'm ready to be interrogated.'

'Tell me why you don't think Rod could've killed his wife and child. He was an alcoholic and a drug user and has a history of violence.'

She wiped up some soft cheese with a chunk of bread and ate it slowly, giving herself time. When she'd swallowed she said, 'I had him under hypnosis a couple of times. It's not infallible of course, but I questioned him on that subject. He didn't do it.'

'You said there was something else troubling him.'

'Well, this is an interpretation rather than something established. He believed he'd killed them but in my opinion that was a sort of cover for something else he either knew or suspected, but couldn't admit to himself.'

'Like?'

'You're the detective, Let's hear from you.'

'He knew who *had* killed them and . . . shut it out.'

She plastered a piece of bread with sun-dried tomato and olive paste and smoothed it off with a forefinger. Longish, pink-painted nails. 'Psychiatry is a speculative business, like a lot of science.'

'Is that a yes or a no, Jerry?'

She leaned into me and kissed my bruised face. 'First intimate use of my name. Progress. It's a maybe, Cliff.'

We did a bit of kissing and groping then and worked on the wine. The coffee machine sparked up and the brewed smell of good, fresh beans wafted through and somehow broke the mood which might have been leading to another trip down the passage. Powerful things, smells.

She broke away and headed for the coffee. 'Next question.'

'Did Rod ever talk to you about a favourite surfing spot? Shit, I mean a surfing spot and a place to take women.'

I watched her closely as she considered this. I wasn't arrogant enough to automatically believe that this highly qualified, sophisticated woman was interested in me, at least not exclusively. She fiddled with the coffee maker for a while, got mugs from a cupboard and seemed to have lost interest in the question until she was sitting back next to me with the mugs, the coffee, a sugar bowl and a cream jug in front of us. She reached out and took my hand and my sun-blasted, thick-knuckled claw looked like a fossil in her smooth, pale fingers.

'I suppose we'll get to the life histories if this goes on. All that shit. But . . . you like me, don't you?'

My voice was thick in my throat. 'I do, Jerry. I find you . . . amazing.'

'Not scary? Not intimidating?'

'No. Why?'

'Men have. I'm glad, Cliff. That's great. Drink some coffee, because you're going to have to drive home tonight. I'll have to look at my files on the computer. I made notes about Rodney and I think there's something in them along those lines — surf and sex. Sit tight.'

She got up and walked away and I watched her. I wasn't drunk; it was long time since that amount of wine could have that effect on me, but I was in a different space from the one I'd inhabited a couple of hours before.

17

Jerry Weir told me that Rodney Harkness had talked about Redhead beach near Newcastle as his favourite place. She got the impression that it was his favourite for more than just surfing. I told her that Glen Withers had lived and worked in Newcastle and had owned a house on the coast.

'That looks like it, then,' she'd said. 'You'll be off up there.'

I said I would. We drank coffee and I could tell it was time to go. We exchanged cards and laughed — not a bad way to finish a meeting like that, with a laugh.

The sight and sound and the smell and the feel of her were filling my mind as I drove away. I was a serial loser in the relationship game but still interested, still hopeful. I went back over the meeting in all its aspects, trying to assess how much hope to invest in it. No conclusions, but it was there and I was happy about it.

I drove to Glebe to check on the house. That didn't take long and I headed back to Bondi, still hoping for a message of some kind from Glen. Happiness is bad for caution and I was driving down Bondi Road before I realised that I'd picked up a tail. I made a few turns and he stayed right with me, doing it well, but there's no such thing as perfect in that business. My first thought was that it was the same interested party that had picked me up when I collected my car. It wasn't a 4WD but that didn't signify. I slowed and he got closer than he should and I caught a glimpse of the registration plate. Couldn't read it but it wasn't smeared over the way it had been on the 4WD. That didn't quite compute. But things were different now — I didn't have Rodney with me and I did have my gun.

I knew Bondi fairly well and knew there were some divided streets that ran on different levels and some dead ends. I turned a few more times until he must have suspected that I was on to him, and then took a long straight, purposeful-seeming run. It brought me out in the split-streets area. One I remembered ended in a small park, but if you didn't know that you'd think it continued on at the higher level. I drove down it fast and he was slow to make the turn. I stopped ten metres short of the barrier, pulled in and killed the lights.

The other car came on, moving quickly and there was a squeal as he hit the brakes. He started to make a U-turn but I started up, gunned the motor and swung forward to block him. I took the .38 from the recessed clamp under the dashboard and jumped out, holding the gun low and close to my leg. I got to the car, a late model Commodore, in a few strides and wrenched the door open.

'Out!'

A big, heavily built man in a suit, with thin, greying hair, clean-shaven, climbed slowly from the car, reaching inside his jacket as he did so.

I brought the gun up. 'Don't.'

He continued the movement and produced a police warrant card, holding it up for me to see the way they do. 'I'd put that thing away if I was you, Hardy. I'm Kevin Sherrin.'

I recognised him then. He was Glen's ex-husband and a Superintendent the last I'd heard of him. I lowered the gun and backed off a step.

'Why were you following me?'

He flipped the folder closed and put it away. 'First things first. Where's Glen?'

'What's it to you?'

'Watch yourself. I can think of three or four charges to pull you in on. I've got some papers Glen has to sign. To do with joint property. Nothing heavy. I've been fucking ringing and emailing her and I've been to the house. No sign of her. Someone told me she was working with you, so I . . .'

'You picked me up in Glebe, right? Why didn't you just come in? Why the tail?'

'That's what I was going to do. But you were in and out too quick. Also you looked like you had something important on your plate.'

It didn't take long to decide to talk to him. Glen hadn't told me much about their split but she hadn't bad-mouthed him. She'd taken it hard and it had led to her drinking problem, but she'd never blamed Sherrin. And the way things stood, a policeman could be useful.

'We can't talk here in the middle of the road. I'm staying at a flat close by. Follow me there and we can discuss it.'

'D'you know where she is?'

I turned away and said over my shoulder, 'No, but I'm as keen to find her as you are. Keener.'

I drove to the flat with the Commodore close behind. No sign of the Pajero. Sherrin parked in the street and followed me up the stairs. The splintered door didn't escape his notice.

'What's this?'

I didn't answer. I was weary and needed a piss and a drink. We went inside. I switched on the light and the first thing Sherrin took in was the bloodstain.

'Jesus, Hardy. What the fuck's been happening? Has Glen been here?'

In the light I could see that he was florid and overweight with puffy features. He still had the tough cop manner, but not the presence to go with it.

'Yes. Give me a minute and I'll tell you about it. First I have to have a piss. D'you want a drink?'

'No.'

'Good. Because one's all I've got. Hang on.'

I emptied my bladder, washed my hands and face and came back into the living room. Sherrin was examining the bloodstain.

'Whose is this? Not Glen's?'

'A junkie who broke in here.'

A nod. 'The door.'

'No. The junkie reckoned the bloke who did

that looked like a cop.'

'What game are you playing, Hardy?'

I went to the kitchen and put the rest of the whisky in a glass and added water. I went back, invited him to sit down and started talking.

I finished my explanation and the drink simultaneously. Sherrin had listened without interrupting.

'Sure you've got nothing else to drink?'

'Not a drop. Coffee.'

He loosened his tie. 'Maybe later. I don't think I've ever heard of a bigger cock-up.'

'I'm inclined to agree.'

'You're inclined to agree. Fuck you. What're you going to do about it?'

'I'm going to try to find them.'

'What about this arsehole who's out to knock Harkness?'

'I'm in the bloody dark about him. I can't seem to find a motive or a suspect. I had an interest in an ex-cop named Doug Schirer for a while, but he's half blind. That reminds me, though.' I flipped through my notebook until I found the name Billy Parkinson, a crim Rod had named as being on Schirer's books. Worth a try. I gave the name to Sherrin who shook his head.

'Billy's dead. Lung cancer got him last year.'

'Scratch him then. Like I told you, if it's the man who broke in here he's been described as looking like a cop by someone who knows what cops look like.'

'Fuck of a lot of good that is.'

Suddenly he looked very tired and distressed

and I wished I had a drink to give him. It occurred to me that he wasn't just looking for Glen to sign papers. I put that to him and he took a long time to answer.

'I want her back,' he said.

'Are you sure?'

'My life's turning to shit without her.'

In my experience lives turn to shit because of the people living with them and there's not much other people can do about it. But I made sympathetic noises. He got up and paced around the room. While he paced I made some coffee and brought it in. He'd calmed down a bit.

'I want to help. I can put a word out up Newcastle way for one thing.'

'All right. I'm going up there tomorrow.'

'I'm tied up on this fucking Internal Affairs course or I'd go myself. But I can see that people up there know about you. Plus I can get a car to come by here from time to time to keep an eye on you.'

'No, don't do that. I'm hoping this bloke will take a run at me. There's no way he can have any better idea of where they are than we do. I don't want him scared off.'

He drained his coffee without appearing to taste it and looked at me. 'How do you figure that?'

'Look, if he's a policeman he can find out who this Glen who left the note is.'

He was so tired he could hardly think. 'How?'

'Cops keep an eye on us. We know that. You knew Glen and I had worked together before and could be again. So could he. If he knows that, he knows about Newcastle. Glen's father was on the job there the same as her. That's easy to find out. If he knows Harkness he could know about his liking for Redhead beach, so . . .'

'Who told you that by the way?'

'I'm not saying.'

'Hardy, I could make a lot of trouble for you.'

'You could, but you won't. We're on the same side.'

'So I'm relying on you to find her and to deal with this joker if he's tagging along.' He tapped the side of his head, indicating where I was carrying the marks of my encounter with Craig. 'I'm not sure that's such a good bet.'

'I don't like it much myself. Got a better idea?'

'I'll work on it.' He took a card from his wallet and dropped it on the table. 'Give me your mobile number in case I need to get in touch. Here's mine.'

I gave him a card. He pocketed it and went towards the door. 'One last thing. Was she drinking when you last saw her?'

'No.'

He nodded and walked out. I listened to his footsteps retreating and when I heard the engine of the Commodore start up and the car move away I went down and retrieved the Smith & Wesson.

I thought about driving to Newcastle and starting to search for Glen and Rod at first light the next day but I decided against it. The way I felt I'd be lucky to make it to Gosford. I was just about to pack it in when I heard a quiet knock at the door. I grabbed the pistol and held it behind my back as I opened the broken door with my left hand.

Craig stood there. He had a bandage around his head like a footballer sent off to the blood bin and his grin was uncertain. I was so surprised to see him that I let my hand come forward and he saw the gun.

'Jesus, man. I . . .'

'It's all right, just being cautious. What do you want?'

'I . . . ah, got something might interest you, like.'

'Like what?'

'Information.'

'Go on.'

'I seen that guy again. That cop.'

I stepped aside and beckoned him in. 'I wonder if I believe you.'

'It's fair dinkum and I got the licence number. I figured it'd be worth something to you.'

'How much were you thinking?'

'Twenty bucks?'

I took a twenty from my wallet and gave it to him. He recited the licence and I scribbled it down. 'When did you see him and what did he do?'

'He didn't do nothing, just drove past slow like. Woulda been five o'clock about. Near that. I haven't got a watch.'

'Red Camry?'

'Yeah.'

'Did you see the bloke who was here just now?'

He hesitated, not knowing whether to lie or not. 'Yeah. I was looking out for you.'

'He's a cop.'

He edged towards the door. 'This bloke's younger and fitter. But that's a few too many cops around for my liking.'

'I can imagine. You any good with your hands, Craig?'

'Not bad. Why?'

'I'm going away tomorrow. Might be a few days. Reckon you could fix that lock?'

'Replace it, like? Sure.'

We drove to the nearest open convenience store and I bought a new lock and screwdriver — $120 all up.

Back at the flat I gave him another twenty. 'Okay, here's what you do. Put the new lock on and find a half brick or something and put the keys under it in the carport. Soon as I'm gone.'

'Great. Yeah, okay.'

I gave him my card. 'If you see that bloke again call me on my mobile. And Craig — don't make a copy of the key.'

He put the card in the pocket of his shirt, the one that had a button, and buttoned it up. Then he shook his head and took off. If Glen and Rod came back before I did they wouldn't be able to get in. Well, stuff them.

18

I wasted time in the morning trying to get in touch with my contact at the DMT. I ring him and give him a number or numbers. He rings me back on a pay phone and gives me a name or names and an address or addresses. I pay money into his TAB account. Recently he's gone part-time at the job, probably because he can afford to on the strength of the kickbacks from people like me. He wasn't available so I'd have to wait on that.

At least on the drive north I'd know to look out for a red Camry. A light-coloured 4WD would be harder, but if I spotted one with a smeared number-plate I'd sit up and take notice. As it was, no show.

Glen had had a house overlooking one arm of Dudley beach when I'd met her. We'd spent some time together there over the next couple of years. Good house. Biggish old fibro place on a large block. One of a set of similar places just a short walk from the water. I knew she'd sold it some time back when she married Sherrin, but I thought she might have cruised past for old time's sake and if someone spotted her I'd have a confirmation that she was in the area. I drove through Whitebridge where I used to walk to get the morning paper and some light exercise. It hadn't changed much. The earthquake damage hadn't reached out this far and developers hadn't intruded.

The street where Glen's house was situated was a different story. A couple of the sturdy, no-nonsense places had gone to be replaced by brick monstrosities with pillars. Glen's place had survived, but from the look of the area it was only a matter of time. I stopped, got out of the car and stretched. The day was hot, a shorts, sandals and T-shirt day, and I was in long trousers, shoes and a business shirt. I could smell the sea and felt a strong gust of nostalgia sweep over me, remembering the good times we'd had up here. Maybe Glen and Rod were having similar good times. I hoped so, but somehow I doubted it.

I looked the houses over, wondering which was the best bet. No contest. Two houses along from Glen's was another survivor with a low fence and the sort of garden that needs care and attention. A woman wearing a man's shirt with the long sleeves buttoned, loose pants and a wide-brimmed hat was giving it just that. She was weeding a flower bed and a watering can stood nearby; a green plastic hose snaked away to a tap at the side of the house. I remembered her from the time I'd spent here but the name had gone. I searched my memory for it as I adjusted my sunglasses and walked towards her. As sometimes happens, the name jumped out at me as I reached the front gate.

'Mrs Reid.'

I was twenty metres away and she didn't hear me. I got ready to shout but a small white dog came bounding up and barked shrilly. Mrs Reid straightened up slowly as befitted her years and peered at me.

'Quiet, Buster. Yes?'

'Could I have a word with you?'

As I recalled she was a widow with a lot of children and grandchildren who were frequent visitors. They parked their cars in the driveway and on the nature strip, two and three abreast, but there were none around now. She patted the dog and it trotted quietly beside her as she came up to the gate.

I took off the shades. 'You might remember me, Mrs Reid. I used to spend some time up here with Glen Withers.' I pointed to the house.

She was seventy plus but straight backed and clear eyed. Her skin was lined and wrinkled, more from smiling than frowning. She wore gardening gloves and carried a trowel. 'You're not the one she married though.'

'No, that was someone else. I was wondering if you'd seen her lately.'

Her faded blue eyes went shrewd. 'Why?'

'It's a long story but I'm looking for her. She's been unwell and having some trouble and . . .'

'I knew it. I remember you now. You got my grandson Eddy's car started one time. Clint.'

'Cliff. I'd forgotten that. You've seen her, haven't you?'

She nodded. 'I always liked Glen and it was nice having a policewoman so close. Yes, I saw her the other day and I knew things weren't right.'

'Why's that?'

'I was sorry to see it. They drove up in one of those big cars and they got out. I was inside but I could see them. She pointed the house out to this man she was with. Younger than her, but a bit old for surfing. There was a big surfboard on the car.'

'But what was wrong?'

'I'd say they were both drunk.'

That was the easy bit. After that it got harder, as I knew it would. I hung around Redhead beach but there was no sign of Glen's car. I asked at the beach kiosk with no result. I checked all the motels within striking distance of the beach and learned nothing. I stayed in the cheapest motel I could find in the area and it wasn't all that cheap. After three days of this I was running low on money with not a lot in my savings account and just about full credit cards. Still no luck with the DMT.

It wasn't all slog. I swam a few times and thought again about moving out of Sydney, going north. Up where I was, less than 200 kilometres north of the big smoke, the air begins to take on a tropical tang and the long beaches seem to promise longer summers and shorter winters than down south. I like the palm trees. The impulse to move grips me from time to time and I've almost yielded to it once or twice. Almost. One night I phoned Jerry and reported on my lack of progress. She was sympathetic. Talking to her tended to push thoughts of leaving Sydney aside.

I wondered how Rod and Glen were doing for money. Rod must have shelled out a bit for his computer and the clothes and other bits and pieces he'd bought. Glen's finances were always rocky. If they were drinking they'd go through a bit in a hurry. I decided to lower my sights and try the caravan parks. I worked north towards Newcastle, west towards Lake Macquarie and then south. I got tired of the sound of my own voice reciting the registration number of the car and the descriptions of Glen and Rod. I got even sicker of the shaken heads, the hostile looks, the air of defeat that hung around some of the establishments.

I pulled into the Ti-Tree Tourist Park near Belmont, which looked to me as if it should have been named the Lantana. This was the lowest on the scale so far. Travelling caravans seemed to be few and the couple of mobile homes that were anchored and hooked up to power and water were faded and tattered. A couple of free-standing cabins had roofs covered in leaves and fallen branches with grass sprouting knee-high in spots the mower couldn't touch.

The fat woman in the office was barely awake in the hot little room, just awake enough to swat at the flies that clustered round the spilt food on her dress. There was a battered soft drink vending machine in one corner of the room and a show-case of sweets and chewing gum on the counter. A waste paper basket held a collection of wrappers from Snickers and Mars Bars and a few Coke cans. I went through my spiel, expecting the usual response.

'Fuck me!' she spat and the flies buzzed away. 'Did I see them? You fuckin' bet I seen them. They did a flit owing us money. Pair of drunks, I shoulda known better.'

I nodded. 'I thought you'd take the money up front.'

'Yeah, well I took her credit card like a mug, and then the phone went out 'cause some fucker put a backhoe through the cable. When I got on to check it was . . . how d'you call it?'

'Dishonoured.'

'Right. Dis-fuckin'-honoured is right.'

No point asking her where they went. I was puzzling what to do about it when she volunteered some more.

'They tried to sell their fuckin' surfboard. One of the permanents here told me. If I'd known they was that broke . . .'

'Did he buy it?'

She laughed, lifted a rolled-up magazine from under the counter and dealt death to a fly. 'Gotcha! Ernie? No way. But he told them they could sell it at Blue Waves at Broken Beach. Good board it was. You after them for money, too?'

'That's right. You say they were drinking?'

'Haven't cleaned out the bottles yet.'

'When was this?'

'Didn't I say? Yesterday, last night.'

Broken Beach was an indentation on the long sweep of beach south of Swansea. It was late afternoon when I got there but still warm and there were still surfers in the water and people on the beach. The place consisted of a collection of shops tucked back from the highway with a couple of pubs and several motels. The surf shop was wide-fronted with boards on display out on the footpath and its name picked out in an arrangement of surf and boogie boards mounted on the roof. Not tasteful, but different.

I parked rear to kerb outside and went in. The music, held down just below deafening, sounded like a combination of Beach Boys and rap. There were surfboards on racks and stands from floor to ceiling and displays of wetsuits and swimsuits and all the other equipment that goes with the cult. Three or four young men in T-shirts and board shorts were wandering around inspecting the goods while another, scarcely older and dressed the same, kept a watchful eye on them.

I approached a tall man with shoulder-length hair that had been red but was bleached and leached by sun and salt water. Wordlessly, I showed him my licence and mimed turning down the music. He reached under the counter and dropped the noise a few decibels.

'You buy boards?' I said.

He fiddled with his earring. 'Sometimes, not that much. What've you got?'

'Not me. I'm looking for someone.' I described Rod and the board and made it clear I wasn't interested in the item, just the seller.

'Yeah,' he said. 'Good board. Hardly been wet. I'll move it. Be better in someone else's hands than his, that's for sure.'

'Why d'you say that?'

'Bloke was a bit pissed and I could smell dope on him, too. I . . . you know, wondered if he'd nicked it, but he had the receipt and everything. Just said he was too old for riding. Thought he'd give it a go again but he was past it. Roger there,' he pointed to the assistant, 'saw him pull up in a Pajero with a woman, so he wasn't a deadbeat or anything. Spoke well and that. She showed us a driver's licence.'

'This was when?'

'First thing this morning. I saw them drinking in the Sea Breeze this arvo. Probably staying there. Should, anyway, they were that pissed.'

'How much did you give him for the board?'

'Fair price. Four hundred. I'll get five. Business. Speaking of which . . .'

'Bluey?'

'Yes, Rog?'

With a wetsuit vest in each hand, Roger had escorted one of the customers to the counter. I thanked Bluey and left the shop. The music hotted up as I reached the footpath.

The Sea Breeze was the furthest away of the two hotels but only a hundred metres or so and I set out for it. Two men stepped out from a fast-food shop doorway and blocked my path.

'Mr Hardy?'

I was anxious to get to the hotel and I side-stepped and tried to keep moving. 'That's right.'

'Just a minute, sir. We'd like to have a word with you.'

19

They introduced themselves as detectives, Loomis and Price from Swansea who'd been contacted by Kevin Sherrin. They bought me a coffee in the fast-food joint and we sat down at a bench under an awning on the footpath. Loomis, the older of the two, lit a cigarette.

'Understand you're looking for Kevin's missus?'

'His ex, yeah, that's right.'

'Having any luck?'

I shook my head.

'Mind telling us what you were doing in the surf shop?'

I had to think fast. If Rod was drinking there was a better than even chance he'd meet any challenge with violence. If he had dope on him he could be in more trouble than he was already. If he and Glen were still holed up in the hotel, the last thing I needed was the company of this pair.

'Bloke's a surfer,' I said. 'I was just asking where the best waves were around here.'

Price grinned. 'And what did you learn?'

'I was told right here.'

Loomis nodded. 'That'd be Bluey, all bullshit. Is there anything we can do to help you?'

'Don't think so, thanks. I was just going to have a drink at the pub over there and keep looking. Only one drink, mind. Which one d'you recommend?'

'The Sea Breeze,' Loomis said.

Price said, 'The Commercial.'

I finished the coffee and fiddled with the styrofoam cup. 'Might have to make it two drinks, then. Thanks for the coffee. I'll tell Kevin you made the offer.'

'Do that,' Loomis said. They got up and moved away. I watched them, praying they wouldn't check on my story in the surf shop. I breathed easier when I saw that in the time we'd been talking the place had closed. I set off for the Sea Breeze and took a quick look back when I was halfway there. No cops in sight.

The Sea Breeze was a low, rambling fifties-style building in cream brick with some later additions in red brick. Small windows in the older part, more glass in the new bit. First stop was the car park and there was no sign of the Pajero. I swore and then spotted a sign indicating the residents' car park. I dodged around a couple of cars pulling out and followed the sign around the side of the building. The residential section, a row of six units, was at the back built in the red brick style and was a motel to all intents and purposes.

The Pajero stood outside the third door from the left but it didn't look much like the vehicle

I was used to. It was dusty and travel-stained and there were severe dents in the front left mudguard and rear right, and a long scrape down the passenger side. The rear-vision mirror on that side was missing and the radio aerial stood at a crazy angle. I took a look inside. The interior was a mess of clothes, bottles, cans and fast food containers.

'Glen,' I said. 'This isn't you.'

I tried the handle of the motel room door and it swung in. The curtains were drawn over all windows and the room was dark. I peered into the gloom with my damaged slow-to-adjust-to-a-change-of-light vision.

The room smelled of alcohol and sweat and marijuana. Glen lay naked on the bed on her back, her pale breasts flat on her chest and her mouth open so that she snored slightly. Rod was fully dressed and sitting on the end of the bed rolling a joint. The ceiling fan was making an insistent hum and I'd opened the door quietly so that he hadn't noticed. His movements had the clumsiness that comes with being stoned or drunk or both and paying too close attention to what's being done.

He hadn't had a shave in a while and his hair was matted and hanging in his eyes, not a help to the joint rolling. I stepped inside and spoke quietly.

'Rod.'

He reacted as if a cannon had gone off in the room. His fist closed around the makings and he sprang to his feet. His eyes were wide and mad in his contorted face and saliva bubbled around the corners of his mouth as he gaped at me. It looked as if he didn't recognise me.

'It's Cliff, Rod.'

He let out a roar, part pain, part anger, part fear, and rushed towards me. I was caught in the narrow opening between the door and a breakfast table and had nowhere to go. He dropped his shoulder and hit me mid-chest with all his weight and leverage and momentum. I was thrown back against the half-open door. My head jerked back and smacked full square into the heel of the door. I heard the sound and felt the impact, but then everything slid away into a reddish haze as my knees gave way and the floor rushed up to meet me.

I wasn't fully unconscious but close to it, too close to move or speak and my eyes kept fluttering closed. I was aware of sounds and movement, but my chest hurt and I was fighting for breath. I realised that I was lying face down and that years of ingrained stink from the synthetic carpet was filling my nostrils. I rolled over. Everything hurt but I could breathe and I managed to keep my eyes open. Turning my head to the side was agony but I did it. Glen was still on the bed. She hadn't moved, but Rod had gone.

Good, I thought. *Go where you like, you fucker. I'm finished with you.*

When I could suck in a full breath I decided that I didn't have any broken ribs, cracked at worst. I levered myself up against the table until

I was sitting. I remembered reading somewhere that with a fractured skull you get bleeding in the ears. Feeling silly, I probed them with a finger. Nothing. I reached gingerly to the back of my head and felt the blood in my hair and the tenderness underneath it. How do they check if a footballer's concussed? Ask him if he knows what day it is. I thought I did. I was pretty sure.

After a while I crawled across to the bathroom, pulled myself upright and used a towel to clean the back of my head. It was still bleeding and I held the towel hard against it until it stopped. I washed my face and hands and looked at myself in the mirror. *You've looked better*, I thought. *And you've looked a hell of a lot worse.* I drank some rusty tasting water that gave me an idea. Clutching at uprights I worked my way back into the room. An uncapped bottle of the Black Douglas sat on the bedside table near Glen's outstretched hand, along with two grimy glasses. I wiped the top on my sleeve and took a swig. It tasted better than the rusty water, much better. I took another swig and felt the warmth run through me, past the aching chest to my still wobbly legs. It didn't do anything for the pain in my head, but you can't have everything.

I put the bottle down and sat on the bed next to the woman I'd once shared just about everything with. The sheets were a tangled mess, stained with sweat and spilled liquor. Her mouth was closed now and she'd stopped snoring, but her immaculate grooming had vanished and she looked ten years older than when I'd last seen her.

Her hair was disordered, greasy and dull, and her skin was dry and flaky. I reached out and put a strand of hair back somewhere near where it belonged.

'It'll be all right, Glen,' I said. 'It'll be all right.'

Slowly and painfully I tidied the room, hanging up clothes and emptying bins. I rinsed the streaky glasses, got rid of the roaches and threw out the bottles and cans. I opened a window to disperse the dope fumes. I wet a towel and bathed Glen's face and wiped the sweat from her body. She stirred but still didn't wake up. I straightened the sheet under her as best I could and covered her with the top sheet. Glen's overnight bag and laptop were in the closet and her handbag was beside the bed. There was no sign of a bag for Rod or any of his clothes.

The effort made me dizzy. I sat and waited for the spell to pass. It took a while, quite a while.

When I felt steady I found Kevin Sherrin's card in my wallet and dialled his mobile.

'Sherrin.'

'This is Hardy. I've found Glen. I've got her with me now.'

'Is she all right?'

'Yes and no. She's been on a bender. She's sleeping it off.'

'What about the bloke?'

'He took off.'

There was a pause and I thought he was going to ask about the how and why of that. I was glad he didn't. 'Where are you?'

'Broken Beach, that's . . .'

'I know where it is. I'm coming up.'

'What about your course?'

'Fuck it. I'll be there by midnight, depending on the traffic. Where are you exactly?'

I told him. I didn't particularly want him to come but clearly there was no stopping him and Glen was going to need someone around for all the pain and guilt and horror she was going to suffer. She was still sleeping soundly so I slipped out, walked back to my car and drove it to the room, parking it where the Pajero had been. There were paracetamol tablets, a toothbrush and toothpaste in my bag. I had a shower, changed my shirt and took three of the tablets with another slug of Scotch. The wound on the back of my head had stopped bleeding but it was throbbing. My chest and left side were bruised where Rod's shoulder had hit me.

I got a can of Coke, a container of orange juice and a sandwich from vending machines near the units and called it dinner. Then I slumped in a chair beside the bed and fell into a doze.

'Rodney!'

I hurt my head against the back of the chair as Glen's voice jerked me awake. She was sitting up, gripping the sheet and staring wildly around her. The room was dark with just a dull glow coming from the bathroom. I went across to the bed.

'Glen, it's Cliff.'

'Cliff. Oh God. Oh God. What? Where's Rodney?'

'He's gone. Lie back. Take it easy.'

'Gone? What do you mean, gone?'

'In the Pajero.'

She fell back against the pillows. 'He's a terrible driver. He'll kill himself.'

Good riddance, I thought.

Her eyes closed and I thought for a moment she'd fallen asleep but she said, 'I feel like death. I wish I was dead. I wish I was dead.'

'You don't. You'll be okay. Just take it a step at a time. Can you make it to the shower?'

'I'm not sure.'

I'd put the Scotch out of sight in my bag but I had the pain-killers to hand. I broke two out of the foil and gave them to her with a glass of water. She swallowed them down and lay back limply. 'We drank and drank.'

'I know. But it's over now. You kicked it once, you can do it again.'

'I don't know.'

She was negative, passive, compliant. I got her to the shower, stripped the cover from the soap and unscrewed the top of the miniature shampoo bottle. She was in there a long time; too long. I went in and she was just standing under the lukewarm water, staring at the tiles. I turned the water off, dried her and got her into the kimono she used as a dressing-gown. In the kimono, with a towel around her hair, she looked something like the Glen I knew. All except her eyes, and they were dark, hopeless hollows.

20

Glen drank four cups of milky, sweet tea, using all the sachets the management provided. She also ate the two lots of biscuits. She dressed in jeans and a sloppy joe, used the hair dryer and we went for a walk on the beach as we'd done often before on a similar beach not many kilometres north. But this was different; we weren't lovers now and never would be again. The question was, where was she going from here?

We took off our shoes and paddled along in the shallows. There was just enough moon and starlight for me to see by. The water was cold but Glen didn't seem to notice.

'I needed someone,' she said. 'I just couldn't go on alone. And I thought he might be the right person, having some of the same problems.'

The water was too cold for me and I steered her onto the sand but I let her keep talking.

'I gave him the computer lesson and he took to it quickly. He's very bright. Then we made love. He was good at that as well. I was happy for the first time in ages. I felt strong, in control.'

My feet were freezing. We stopped and sat

down and I put my shoes and socks on. She didn't. She hugged herself as if to keep warm although the air wasn't that cold. I thought it might be the beginning of the shakes that were bound to come, but it wasn't.

'So we went out and had lunch and it all felt so normal and nice. I felt normal and nice. Like an ordinary person, not like a fucking alcoholic.'

'So you had a drink.'

'Two. We had two glasses of house white each. But Rodney bought a bottle of Scotch when I wasn't looking and we started in on that when we got back to the flat. Then it seemed like a good idea to go away for a while, to forget about all this shit. So we did. We collected some of my clothes and took off. He said Redhead beach was one of his favourite places in the world. And I said . . .'

I knew how it would have gone. Swapping stories, finding parallels, drawing closer until it seemed it was all meant to be. And the alcohol would have helped, broken down barriers, released inhibitions, provided punctuation points; lubricated the possibilities.

The shakes started with the tears and she sank to her knees on the sand. I put my arm around her and felt the convulsions surge through her and heard her grinding her teeth. The spasm didn't last long and she wanted to walk again. Standing up made me grunt with the pain in my chest and side. Glen didn't notice. We went back the way we'd come and she told me how the money had started to run out, partly through Rod buying dope, and how they'd ended up broke in the Ti-Tree caravan park. How Rod had insisted on driving and banged up the car.

We found a Nite Owl shop and bought more tea bags, Coca-Cola and chocolate — comfort food. On the way we began to talk about the Harkness case. I told her what had happened at my end, including my encounter with Warren and my suspicions about why he and his mother had hired us.

'Bastards,' Glen said. 'Anyway, I suppose we're off it now.'

'I don't know. Don't answer if you don't want to, but did you get anything out of him about what sent him off the rails. Did he say anything about killing his wife and child?'

I'd told her about getting this information from the ex-cop Hughes and Jerry Weir and how this had upped the concern for her safety being felt by me and Kevin Sherrin. She'd taken it on board, including the mention of Sherrin, without much reaction. She was still trapped by her own demons. But she answered the question.

'No. Nothing like that. But he hated her. She was promiscuous. I located an old girlfriend of hers who gave me a list of her lovers. I've got it on file. God, that reminds me. Rodney dropped my laptop. I have to see if it's still working.'

A good sign that, concern about possessions. We hurried back to the units. Glen pulled the computer out, unzipped the bag and turned it on. It booted up smoothly and the screen glowed. Glen sat back.

'That's good. For what it's worth.'

'You'd better check that you can access the files.'

She tapped away and a file came up. I leaned over her shoulder.

'What's this?'

'It's that list of names I told you about — blokes who'd fucked Lucille.'

I ran my eye down the list. There were seven names — Lucas, MacDonald, Bartoli, Ellsworth, Seagram, Sexton — none of them meant anything to me. Glen turned the machine off and put it back in its case without bothering to close the zipper. Her eyes were set in that hopeless, far-seeing, looking-at-nothing gaze.

I hadn't told her about Sherrin coming up. Maybe this was the time. 'Glen, Kevin Sherrin's on his way here. Should arrive soon.'

She sat on the bed with her shoulders hunched. 'Why?'

'He cares about you.'

'Could've fooled me. No, that's not true. He's a good man, Kevin. The only thing wrong with him is that bloody job. Have you ever thought about it, Cliff? What this sort of work does to people? The crap we see. The lies we listen to. The shit that bubbles up from down below.'

I put the jug on and got set to make tea for her and coffee for me. I tossed her a chocolate bar and she let it fall on the bed. 'I try not to think that way,' I said. 'Sometimes we help get things straightened out.'

'Not often.'

She was determined on sliding down and there

wasn't a lot I was going to be able to do about it. I made the drinks and put them on the table, forcing her to get off the bed at least, stand upright, take in a breath. She reached down and picked up the chocolate, ripped it open and ate a couple of squares. Still standing, she drank some tea and pulled a face.

'Shit,' she said, 'shit, shit, shit. I want a real drink.'

As if on cue, a knock came on the door. I opened it and Sherrin, in his suit but looking weary, walked in.

'Hello, Kev,' Glen said. 'Wouldn't a have a drink on you, would you?'

Sherrin looked at me.

'A bad patch,' I said. 'She'll get through it.'

'Don't talk about me like that! Maybe *she* won't fucking get through it.'

'I'll take you back to Sydney,' Sherrin said. 'You can go to an AA meeting as soon as we get there.'

'At three a.m?'

'Yes, at three a.m.'

Glen squared her shoulders and looked from one of us to the other as if she was seeing us for the first time. But at least she was seeing us and the blank state had gone. I got some inkling of the power of the AA approach. 'Okay,' she said. 'Yes, I think that'd be best. I think it's that or . . .'

'A day at a time,' Sherrin said.

Glen shook her head as she picked up her handbag and zipped the laptop bag shut. 'The way I feel it's an hour at a time.'

I carried her overnight bag out to Sherrin's car,

a white Pulsar, and we stood around in the cool night air trying to find something to say. Eventually Sherrin couldn't hold it in any longer. 'What about this bloke?'

'I'll look for him,' I said.

He looked at my Falcon and the three other cars lined up at the units. 'He's stolen Glen's car, right? I could put out a call on him.'

'Don't do that,' Glen said. 'I let him drive it. You could say he's just . . . borrowed it.'

Plus, I thought, *he's drunk, hasn't got a licence and has marijuana on him.* If the cops caught him he was headed back to the institution and that didn't suit me. I wanted to find out what was behind all this crazed behaviour, whether it worked out well for Warren St John and his bitch of a mother or not.

Glen rubbed her eyes and shivered. 'Cliff, I can't go on with this.'

'I'll see what I can do. I'll talk to the brother. Don't worry. Just get yourself together again. We'll see how it works out.'

She got into the car and sat straight, looking pale and fragile through the tinted glass.

Sherrin said, 'Thanks, Hardy.'

We didn't shake hands, as if we both sensed it would make Glen look like some kind of goods, handed over. He drove off and I went into the unit and dug out the Black Douglas. About two inches left. I poured it out and added an ice cube. I kicked off my shoes, dimmed the lights and sat on the bed, propped up against the pillows, to drink it but I was asleep after two sips.

21

The insistent ringing of my mobile woke me. It was close to 4 a.m. so I'd had about three hours sleep, enough to make me dopey and slow to respond but not enough to be refreshing. I fumbled for the phone, knocked it to the floor and swore several times before I was able to answer.

'Yes. Who's this?'

'Cliff, it's Jerry. Where are you?'

That got my attention. I swallowed the rest of the drink and tried to clear my head. 'Jerry. I'm up Newcastle way still. What's happening.'

'Oh God, I hoped you were closer. Rod's been here. It was . . . terrible.'

'Are you all right? Did he hurt you?'

'Yes, a bit. He tried to kill me, I thought. He was drunk and crazy. He . . .'

'Are you safe now? Are you locked in?'

'Yes, yes. I'm safe, but I don't understand. He was raving about you and this woman, Glen and his wife.'

'Stay put. I'm on my way. I'll be there in a couple of hours, say three.'

'I'm sorry. I . . .'

'It's okay. I'm leaving now. Ring me any time if you need to. I'm coming. Do you need a doctor?'

She almost laughed and the sound made me feel relieved. 'I *am* a doctor. Thanks, Cliff. I'll see you soon then.'

I grabbed the few things I'd taken into the unit, threw them in the car and was off within a couple of minutes. Underfed and underslept, with a dull ache in my head and pain through my upper body, I was in no condition for driving, but the traffic on the highway was light and I made good time. Rod was running out of control but there must have been some reason for him to go to Jerry. Maybe there'd been more between them than she'd let on. I decided not to worry about that and to concentrate on driving.

Dawn broke when I was halfway there and it was fully light by the time I got to Mosman. I went up to the house as quickly as I could, given my battered condition, and rang the bell. Jerry opened the door. She was barefoot, pale and swathed in a black velvet dressing-gown. She had a black eye and a bandaged head and her throat was bruised. She reached for me and wrapped her arms around me. I gave a gasp of pain but grabbed her when she tried to pull away.

'What's the matter?' she said.

I held her and kissed her hair, keeping clear of the bandage. 'I had a run-in with Rod as well. He flattened me. What happened here?'

She drew me inside and closed the door. I examined her injuries in the light flooding in from the skylight. 'Jesus, he throttled you.'

'Tried to. I fought him off. I can fight and I was terrified. Look.' She showed me her right hand. The knuckles were skinned and three of the nails were broken.

'You did better than me. How much damage did you do to him?'

'Not much. Drew a bit of blood from his mouth and I think I loosened a couple of teeth. I got my knee in his groin as well.'

'Good.'

'It seemed to pull him out of his frenzy at least. Then he landed one last swing.' She touched her eye.

We went through to the living room and she noticed the stiffness in my movement. I told her what had happened and she examined the back of my head and made me take off my shirt and breathe in and out.

'We'll mend,' she said. 'But I don't know about him now.'

'Tell me what happened.'

'In a minute. You're going to stay for a while, aren't you?'

'If you want me to.'

'I do. I'll make some tea. Uh, do you drink tea?'

'If you've got some brandy to put in it.'

She made the tea and I spiked mine and she told me that Rod had arrived some time around midnight and hammered on the door. He was drunk and stoned and hysterical and she tried to calm him down but he got more and more worked up. When she mentioned me he assaulted her.

'It wasn't a sexual attack. It was just an assault.

He hit me but there wasn't too much force in it.' She touched her eye, then the bandage. 'I almost ducked under this one. Then he had me by the throat and it got serious. He was raving about you and Glen and his wife.'

I sipped the laced tea and it tasted pretty good and soothing. The only problem was too much soothing and I'd be out on my feet. I struggled to concentrate. 'You're the psychiatrist, what would you say was driving him? Apart from the booze and the dope.'

She considered the question. 'Jealousy.'

I nodded. 'You tell me he hated his wife and I've learned that she had a number of lovers. We've seen how violent he can be and now you say he's subject to jealousy. Have to consider the possibility that he did kill his wife. You said the hypnotism stuff isn't infallible.'

'That's right, but there's something that doesn't fit.'

'I know. The kid. He wouldn't kill the kid.'

'I don't think so, but have you ever heard him talk about her?'

I thought back. 'No, not once.'

'He didn't with me either, or couldn't. It was as if . . .'

I was having trouble staying awake. The brandy had taken the edge off the pain in my head and chest and was beckoning me towards sleep. But Jerry was working at it and I had to try to stay with her. 'As if what?'

'I've done some grief counselling in my time. It seemed to me that Rodney's attitude to his daughter was very like that of people who've lost a child. Refusal to even mention the name isn't uncommon. In some societies it's institutionalised for all sorts of reasons.'

Anthropology was just too heavy for me and I felt my eyes closing. I felt guilty; she'd been knocked around as much as me and had probably had as little sleep. Women are tougher and she was younger. I was dimly aware of my shoes being pulled off and my body being laid out on the couch and something soft being put under my head. That did it. I was gone.

The brandy did a good job. I slept deeply and the dreams I had were those silly, rather pleasant ones that don't make any sense but aren't threatening. I was in the middle of one about building a sandcastle on a beach when Jerry shook me gently awake.

'Cliff, there's a call on your mobile. I answered it because I didn't want it to wake you up but he says it's urgent. You'd better take it.'

I'd put the mobile with my car keys on the coffee table. It was less than a metre from my head but I hadn't heard it ring. I picked it up.

'Cliff, Frank Parker here.'

'Frank? What's up?'

'Where are you?'

'Mosman.'

'Who with?'

'C'mon, Frank. What's this about?'

'You'd better get back to Glebe and go straight to the station. They want to talk to you. Rodney Harkness has been murdered.'

PART 3

22

Rod had been found in Randwick in the workshop of a service station that had been closed pending redevelopment of the site. An attempt had been made to set fire to the building but a heavy shower of rain had prevented the fire getting hold. A Detective Sergeant Lance Matthiesson from the Eastern command was in charge of the investigation and he interviewed me at the Glebe station where I'd reported on Frank's instructions.

Matthiesson was a stocky, no-nonsense type who knew his job. 'The body was identified from the contents of the wallet,' he said. 'We contacted the brother and he told us about you and Glen Withers. I knew you were mates with Parker so I rang him to locate you. Save sending someone round or stopping you on the road.'

That was Matthiesson's style. No bullshit mystifying about how they'd got on to me. A straight answer to a straight question of mine, so I tried another.

'What about Glen?'

'She's very ill apparently. Kevin Sherrin's vouched for her whereabouts last night and he guarantees she'll talk to us as soon as she's fit. You don't look too flash yourself, by the way.'

I'd come straight from Jerry's place and must have looked as bad as I felt. 'I'm okay. Sherrin can vouch for me up to a certain time as well. After that I was on the road to Sydney and then with someone in Mosman.'

'Name?'

'Dr Jerry Weir. She's a psychiatrist who treated Harkness when he was in the bin.'

I gave him the address and he wrote it all down. We were in a corner of the detectives' room and had it pretty much to ourselves, with just the odd person wandering in and out briefly. 'I hope you're going to be as helpful as possible on this,' Matthiesson said.

'How much did Frank Parker tell you?'

'Quite a bit, but I want to hear it all again from you.'

'Fair enough, but first tell me how he was killed.'

The room was getting warm and Matthiesson took off his blazer and hung it over the back of the chair he was using. Plain grey trousers, blue shirt, no tie. Since the latest round of corruption investigations cops have been dressing down. 'It was pretty. He'd been tied to a workbench. Stripped. Bolt-cutters had been used.'

'Not . . .?'

'No. A little finger, part of. Cigarette burns. He'd been tortured, then shot in the head. That must've been welcome.'

'Poor bastard. All right, I'll tell you what I know.'

I ran through it all, sticking to the facts and leaving out things like my speculations about why the Harknesses had hired Glen in the first place. Matthiesson got it all on tape and made notes from time to time as I was talking. He stopped the tape a few times to ask questions; nothing I couldn't answer. As I spoke I realised how badly Glen and I had bungled the assignment and I started to feel a build-up of anger at Rod's torturer and assassin.

'So all you've got on this bloke, if he's the murderer, is that he can shoot a rifle, drives first a 4WD then a red Camry and looks like a cop. No idea of why he wanted Harkness dead?'

I shook my head.

'Did you check on the rego of the Camry?'

I looked innocent.

'C'mon, Hardy.'

'I tried. My source wasn't available.'

'Leave it alone, then. Leave it all alone. Just make sure you're available if needed.'

I said I would be. We didn't shake hands. Maybe handshaking was going out of fashion with cops. I left the station and drove home. The house looked shabby, not up to scratch; the way I felt.

After ten days I was out of the loop. I had a few more sessions with Matthiesson when he tried to pump me for more information. I didn't have much to give him but got a bit more myself. The police hadn't been able to locate Craig, the junkie Mr Fixit. The address he'd given me was either a fake or he'd moved on. I'd told them about the broken door and Craig's repair job and where the key was. They found the key and searched the flat with no result. Rodney Harkness had been abducted somewhere between Mosman and where his body was found. The numberplate on the red Camry belonged to a white Commodore stolen some months back and never recovered, like Glen's Pajero.

Kevin Sherrin had taken some leave and was looking after Glen. I left a phone message of support but I heard nothing back. I got an email which had been sent to Glen and copied to me from Warren Harkness severing all connection, declaring the contract null and void and stating that no money was owing. It was what I expected but, like the whole business, it left a nasty taste in my mouth.

For want of something better to talk about, I told Matthiesson my suspicions about why the Harknesses had instigated the investigation. I had a little support for it in the form of the last of Lucille née Hammond's notes, received almost seven years before Glen was contacted by Warren St John. It seemed to confirm that they were looking to have Lucille and the daughter declared dead.

'Nothing illegal about that,' Matthiesson said.

'No, but they didn't level with us.'

Matthiesson shrugged uninterestedly and I brought up the matter of the suspicions surrounding the old man's death. We were in the pub on the corner of Carlisle and Norton Streets in Leichhardt — I'd just finished my workout and Matthiesson had agreed to meet me there as he had other business in the area. It was 11 a.m. and we were sitting over a couple of judicious light beers on a very hot morning.

Matthiesson took a sip and wiped his mouth. 'Yeah, I looked into that when I was backgrounding this fucking business. The word was the wife had offed him somehow but there was no way to prove it.'

'Nice people.'

'You're thinking Warren got his brother out to get rid of him. Hired Glen to muddy the waters.'

'I hadn't gone quite that far, but what d'you reckon?'

'You know what's against it?'

I took a drink and tried to pretend I enjoyed light beer. 'Yeah, for one thing, Warren claims he resisted his brother's release.'

'Could be lying. I can tell you we drew a complete blank there. That Rutherford joint would hardly tell us a thing and we'd have Buckley's of getting an order to search. From what little they did say, we got the impression that the civil liberties lawyers were acting under confidential instructions from another set of lawyers who were acting blah, blah.'

We both knew what the other objection was but I spelled it out anyway. 'Plus the way he was killed. Tortured for information. It looks personal.'

'Or was made to look that way to deflect attention away from the brother.'

I shook my head. 'Only the hit man would know.'

Jerry used almost the same phrase but with a different spin when we talked it over. 'Only the person who killed him knows what Rodney's secret was. That's assuming he learned it. We'll never know unless he's caught.'

I nodded. 'Seems unlikely.'

'It irks you, Cliff, doesn't it?'

'Everything about the whole bloody business irks me.'

We were in the backyard of her Mosman place in the cool of an evening. We were seeing each other regularly and making love again as soon as our injuries mended. The relationship was going well. We shared some interests — tennis, reading, old films, resolute atheism, Radio National. Our backgrounds were very different; she was the only daughter of a husband and wife doctor team and had disappointed them by not becoming a surgeon after taking her medical degrees. She said she'd rather talk to people than cut them up. Her parents were dead and she owned the house. An early marriage hadn't worked and seeing so many damaged people had made her wary. She was smart and funny and liked a drink and sex. Despite the comfort she'd grown up in and still enjoyed, she was disenchanted left Labor in politics. Full steam ahead, but we both knew that the ghost of Rodney Harkness hovered over us.

We were sitting on old but still solid garden furniture drinking wine. The light was dying and the house was a solid shape against a clear sky. It doesn't get much better than Sydney in mid-Spring.

'Not an auspicious beginning was it?' Jerry said. 'You coming to grill me about a patient and me admitting I'd had an affair with him.'

'And then him knocking both of us about. No, but we're doing all right.'

'Are we? I suppose I shouldn't feel like this, given that what I do doesn't often make for endings of any kind, happy or unhappy, but I'd feel more . . . at ease with you if we knew why.'

'Not who?'

She slapped at a mosquito. 'Not so much that. I'm more interested in the secret that killed him. It must have been . . . potent.'

I remembered that she'd said she was writing a book about people who compulsively confessed and I wondered if her interest was academic. Unworthy thought. I had the same feeling. We needed some closure. A few more mosquitos buzzed in and we gathered up the bottle and glasses and moved towards the house.

'The weird thing is,' I said, 'I have a feeling there's something I know, or I've heard, some connection that could help to make sense of it, but I can't grasp it. You know, like when you can't remember the name of a book or a movie.'

'Keep trying,' she said.

I did try. I read back over my notes many times and tried to recall my conversations with Rod and everyone else in as much detail as I could. There were irritating loose ends. For example, no identification of the bullet that had lodged in the upholstery of my car. Not that it would've helped.

Thoughts of Glen kept intruding. Thoughts of how close we'd been and then how hurt. I wanted to break Sherrin's embargo but I didn't. There was still something that I couldn't put my finger on. I tried the old trick of clearing my mind of everything to do with things Harkness and hoping the thing I was searching for would jump into the space, but no luck.

23

The police released the body and Rodney's funeral was notified in the papers. Jerry and I sent flowers and attended it together. The Harknesses were Catholic apparently, although religion hadn't loomed large for Rod. I'd never heard him mention it and it was news to Jerry.

'Is that unusual?' I'd asked when the funeral notice appeared. 'To be brought up Catholic and not make any reference to it to a shrink?'

'Not these days. Most intelligent lapsed Catholics get rid of it completely.'

But when you're dead you've got no say and the mass with all the trimmings was held in a church in Rose Bay. The attendance was thin with the men in suits looking prosperous and the women in fashionable outfits looking pleased to be dressed up and having something to do. I wore a darkish jacket and trousers. No tie. Jerry was in a trouser suit and flatties. We weren't the only informals. A couple of men of about Rod's age were dressed sober casual and I judged them to be old surfer buddies. A rather scruffy individual with long hair and a wrinkled suit was addressed as Barney by someone and I took him to be Barney Nugent, Rod's one-time agent. Nice of you to come.

Warren St John and Lady Rachel Harkness strutted their stuff in expensive black with Lady R making extensive use of a lace handkerchief and Warren sucking in his gut when he remembered. A little bit of sermonising and hymn singing goes a very long way with me, especially when it's being done for someone who didn't give a toss about it. I fidgeted and Jerry prodded me into line.

I was on the aisle and tried to catch Warren's eye as he filed out as pallbearer. He saw me but he didn't break stride. *What are you thinking?* I thought. *What are you feeling?* I doubted that I'd ever know and it irked me.

As we drove in the procession to Waverley Cemetery, Jerry's Saab not out of place with the Mercs and BMWs, no sign of the surfies, Jerry said, 'Well, did you spot him?'

'Who?'

'The killer. Weren't you looking out for him?'

I shook my head. 'I've never yet known a murderer who turned up at a victim's funeral. Besides, the only description I've got of a possible suspect is that he looked like a cop — suit, moustache, sure of himself. That fitted a few blokes there.'

'So, why did you want to come?'

'Why did you agree to come? You had to cancel two appointments. I had nothing else on.'

She smiled. 'You like to win these little battles, don't you?'

'I don't know. I like the battles.'

We drove on a bit before she answered. 'I felt close to him at one time and then there was that awful scene. I suppose I just didn't want that to be the last memory.'

'Same here.'

There are worse places to finish up than Waverley Cemetery with its old horse troughs out front and its wrought-iron gates. Long time since a horse drank there, but the troughs lend a funny sort of extra dignity to the place, making it feel timeless which, for the residents, it is.

The Harknesses had a family plot in the cemetery. Nothing elaborate compared to some of the Gothic structures striving to be monumental and looking pathetic, but adequate enough to plant a few with space for a few more. We stood well back while they went through the rituals. Barney Nugent hadn't taken this next step and in fact the cortege had been quite small. It didn't take long for the mourners to disperse and the men with the shovels to get to work.

Jerry turned her mobile back on and it rang almost straight away. I wandered forward to inspect the plot. Old Sir Ralph was there along with Wilbur, who I took to be his brother. There was also a Juliet, born 1970, died 1995, beloved daughter of Ralph and Rachel, loved sister of Warren and Rodney.

Jerry finished with her call and joined me. I pointed to the headstone. 'Did Rod ever mention a sister?'

Jerry shook her head. 'Never. I'm beginning to wonder if I knew him at all.'

'Me, too.' I took her arm and steered her away.

She protested. 'I wanted to think about that. Where are you taking me?'

'To meet my mother,' I said.

My mother's grave was in the Protestant section of the cemetery. That would have amused her, as she disliked all religions about equally. She didn't have a view, tucked in as she was behind more imposing headstones and tombs. The headstone was faded and the little fenced plot was overgrown. My sister occasionally came out and cleaned it up, but she obviously hadn't been around for a while.

Ruby Salome Hardy née Kelly, was the daughter of Hannah Lee an Irish gypsy, and her de facto husband Terence Kelly, an Irishman who had several de facto wives and a few families in Ireland and Australia. Hannah had left him and defied Romany tradition by crossing the water to Australia, bringing Ruby and her sister Rona with her. She'd battled all her life and my mother had determined not to live the same way. She was out for a good time, whatever the state of the family finances, and she pretty much succeeded in having one to the despair of my father, who was a sober-sided sixth-generation Australian of French and English extraction. My mother had died early of diabetic complications.

Jerry stood beside me as we looked at the weather-pitted headstone. 'Not a long life,' she said.

'No, but a merry one.'

She hugged my arm. 'That's pretty good if you can remember her that way.'

'I mostly remember her singing and playing the piano when she had a skinful and trying to get sugar into her when she had a hypo. But she was fun. Too much for Dad though.'

'Is he here as well?'

'No. Cremated. Well, there she is. What about yours?'

'Both cremated. Neat and tidy people. We're both orphans. At least you've got a sister. I was an only child. Nieces and nephews, Cliff?'

'One of each and I've got an anti-godson — name of Peter.' I didn't tell her about my recently discovered daughter, Megan. I don't know why. She'd gone to America and didn't look like coming back. I hadn't heard from her for some time.

We walked away from the grave and I told her about Frank Parker and Hilde Stoner and how they'd met and our relationship. I was hot in my jacket and I took it off and slung it over my shoulder. I reached for her hand after that and we walked along between the graves hand in hand, both effectively childless, both end-of-the liners. At least that's what I was feeling and it made me think of Juliet St John Harkness who'd gone unmentioned by her mother and two brothers. I spoke my thought out loud.

'There has to be something to it.'

'You mean the sister? Yes, I was thinking the same thing.'

'I can't stand this,' I said. 'I'm going to have to look into it.'

'Don't you need a client? I mean to cover your costs and give you some . . . authority?'

'Technically, yes.'

'Who've you got in mind?'

We reached the Saab. It wasn't a day for the un-air-conditioned Falcon. I was driving and I used the central locking remote. A childish pleasure in that. I shrugged. 'Dunno.'

'What about me?'

'Come on.'

'I'm serious. I'm still working on that book about confession and Rodney's case is still very, very relevant. I need the data and if you can come up with it from investigating further . . .'

We got into the car and I started the engine. 'Don't patronise me, Jerry.'

She turned towards me with the sort of intensity I'd seen in her on the tennis court and in bed. 'Fuck you. I'm not patronising you. This shit needs sorting out. For my research and for us if we're going to get anywhere.'

The cool air from the vents blew over us and dropped our temperatures. I reached across the space between the bucket seats and smoothed her blue-black hair. 'Okay, okay,' I said. 'You're on. It's two hundred dollars a day plus expenses.'

'Peanuts,' she said. 'Shit, sorry.'

The Saab's engine was silky soft. 'That's okay. I haven't got three university degrees, just half a one.'

'Never too late.'

I gave the car some accelerator and it responded with a healthy surge. 'Not in this life.'

A look into the life and death of Juliet Harkness seemed like a place to start but I was closed off from the primary source of information — Warren and Lady Rachel. To have got some dope on Rod's life's loves Glen must have had a source or sources of some kind so I phoned her.

'Kevin Sherrin.'

'Uh, Kevin, this is Cliff Hardy.'

'Yes.'

'How's Glen?'

'Fragile, what d'you think?'

This wasn't going well. 'Sorry to hear that. Has she spoken to the police?'

'Yes, she's told them everything she can and they've agreed to leave her alone. She needs complete rest and to be free of all this shit. What's this about, Hardy?'

I could tell I wasn't going to get anywhere. 'Nothing, just give her my regards.'

'Will do.'

Quick cut-off. I didn't completely believe Sherrin. The Glen I knew was tougher than that and I guessed that his protectiveness was at least partly for his own purposes. By now he must have used up a fortnight of leave and I wondered if he was still by her side night and day. Only one way to find out,

The next morning at seven I was parked on Glen's street in Paddington. After the break with Sherrin and selling her beach house she bought a tiny Paddington terrace to live in and as a base for her business. With Sherrin in residence it'd be crowded. The narrow street was packed with cars carrying residents' stickers. Sherrin's Pulsar stood outside the house. I squinted and made out a sticker. Looked like Kevin was in for the long haul. The day was going to be hot and I was hoping Sherrin wasn't playing house husband all day long because when the sun got above the rooftops the interior of the Falcon would be a sweatbox. *C'mon, Kev,* I thought. *Go to work.*

At 7.45 Sherrin emerged in his suit and carrying a briefcase. He put on a pair of spectacles, got into his car and drove off. He wasn't going for the paper. I gave him a few minutes just in case he'd forgotten something before crossing the road and walking the fifty metres to the house. Single-storey terrace. Pocket handkerchief front garden, tiled path and porch under a bullnose verandah. Bars on the window. Security door. Intercom. I pressed the buzzer.

'Yes?' Glen.

'Glen, it's Cliff. I need to talk to you.'

'Why didn't you ring?'

'I did. Kevin ran a very strong block. I take it he didn't tell you I rang?'

That was calculated. The Glen I knew wouldn't have liked someone running her life to that extent. I heard her mutter 'Shit', and then the security door clicked and the interior door opened.

She was wearing white silk pyjamas and a white towelling robe and the clothes made her pallor even more noticeable. Her usually stylish hair seemed to be in need of work and her eyes looked to have receded into her skull. She stood aside and beckoned me in.

'I look like shit, I know. You look great. I hear you're fucking the psychiatrist. Nice work.'

I eased past her into the narrow passage. 'Where'd you hear that?'

She shrugged. 'Forget. You might as well come in. I'm working my way through my first pot of coffee. First of ten or so.'

We went through to the kitchen. The back wall had been knocked out and replaced with a floor-to-ceiling window and a sliding glass door so that the light flooded in. The back garden was half as big again as the front, which meant that you could actually sit in it and stretch your legs. The few plants, flowers and vines, looked neglected.

Glen poured coffee and we sat at the small table. Three would have been a crowd. Her every move and gesture was indifferent as if she was only barely there physically and somewhere else entirely mentally. I tried not to appear shocked at her appearance but it was hard. She was maybe ten kilos underweight and, worst of all, her fingernails were bitten down. I'd never known Glen to bite her fingernails.

She held her coffee mug in both hands. 'Don't look at me.'

The coffee was strong and bitter, stomach-scouring stuff. 'I need your help,' I said.

'That's a laugh. Me, help anyone? Still less you. I'm the one who needs help. Lots and lots of help.'

'You're getting it from Kevin, aren't you?'

She was working her way through the coffee quickly. 'Poor Kevin. He's trying so hard, and he's so fucking boring.'

'What have you been doing with yourself?'

'Nothing, just trying not to drink.'

'Maybe you should . . .'

'Don't tell me what I should do. You're sitting pretty — fucking your rich psychiatrist, no doubt with some juicy case to keep you busy.'

I couldn't drink any more of the coffee. I put the mug aside and shook my head. 'No, I haven't got a case, juicy or otherwise. I'm just trying to find out who killed Rod Harkness and why.'

Her head came up and she showed the first sign of interest in anything other than her own misery since I arrived. She got a tissue from the pocket of her robe, blew her nose and ran her hands over her hair. 'Why would you want to do that?'

I shrugged. 'I feel I owe it to him.'

She nodded. 'I can understand that. I suppose I'd feel the same if I let myself.'

It was on the tip of my tongue to tell her to let herself, but I held it back. She smiled at me and 50 per cent of the haggard, drab look vanished. 'I know what you were going to say. I know you, Cliff.'

'And I know you. You'll bounce back from this.'

'You reckon? Well, maybe. Anyway, what can I do?'

I told her about discovering that Rod had had a sister. It was news to her and, as with Jerry and me, it struck her as strange and potentially illuminating.

'Can't talk to the brother or the mother,' I said. 'I was wondering if you got onto anyone in the early stages who might know something about the family. I mean, you seemed to get some good stuff on the wife.'

'I did, didn't I? Not that it went anywhere. Hang on a minute, I'll have a look.'

She got up and went down the passage to the second of the rooms leading off it. Something about her pale feet under the robe struck me as sad. Glen had been a sun lover. By this time of the year she'd usually have a tan like a TV star's. I looked around the small, well-organised and appointed kitchen. Lots of signs of Glen at work — sealed jars containing sugar, pasta, coffee, a metal rack suspended from the ceiling to hang pots and pans on; sink, microwave, dishwasher all fitted in to a space that didn't look big enough to hold them. An open cupboard had two empty shelves, puzzling until I worked it out. The shelves would have held wine glasses and tumblers. Clear the decks.

Glen came back carrying her laptop. She'd put on white jeans and a black T-shirt. She put the computer on the table and went off to the bathroom adjacent to the kitchen. I heard her run water and rattle things. When she came back she'd tidied her hair, washed her face and applied a little makeup. I said nothing as she unzipped the case. She booted up the computer and started clicking.

'I haven't touched this since that night. Seems a long time ago but I suppose it isn't. Time gets all fucked up when you're off the grog.'

'I know what you mean.'

She kept clicking. 'You only sort of know.

Doesn't matter. Okay, here we are. I've got a file on the people I talked to about Rodney's wife. I think there was one . . . This is the one who had the dope on the boyfriends and . . . this one, right, here she is. Birgit Hansen. Now, she went to school with Lucille Hammond and she'd also dated Rodney. Seemed to know a bit about the family. Couldn't stand Warren. She didn't say anything about a sister, but I really didn't have very long with her and she pissed me off.'

'Why was that?'

'She was very, very antagonistic to Rod. Hated him. I didn't find out why but perhaps I know now. I've got her phone number and address here. Another one of Lucille's friends put me on to her.'

I wrote the details down and Glen killed the screen. 'Okay?'

'Thanks, Glen. It could be useful.'

'House calls. That's what we do, isn't it? Make house calls.'

I was glad to hear her say we. 'That's about it. How did you make contact?'

'Just rang her up. She's a wannabe novelist. Couldn't wait to meet a real live detective. But watch yourself when you make this house call.'

'How's that?'

'She's a man-killer, Cliff. Just your type.'

24

Birgit Hansen (I kept thinking she'd have to change her name if she wanted to be a novelist) lived in a block of units in Bondi Junction. It was a bit too close to the freeway for comfort and not high enough to see the water. Still, there were doctors' rooms in the street and it was no distance to the shops. Not cheap to buy or rent. I parked in a two-hour zone and found a phone, not hard in Bondi Junction where they sprout on every corner. It's hard to find a coin operated one though and like the well-prepared detective I had a phone card with plenty of credit. Call me old-fashioned, I still prefer a real phone to my mobile if I have the choice.

'Hello, whoever you are. This is Birgit.'

For a second I thought it was an answering machine but it was the real live woman. 'Ah, Ms Hansen, my name is Hardy. I'm a private detective and an associate of Glen Withers who spoke to you.'

'Oh, yes. The lady without a gun.'

'I'm sorry?'

'I asked her if she had a gun and she said she didn't. Have you got a gun?'

'Not with me. I can get it if I have to.'

She laughed. 'No, that's all right. I . . .'

I knew I had to jump in while she was uppish. 'Ms Hansen, I know it's not your favourite subject but I need to talk about the Harkness family. It's very important but I won't take much of your time.'

There was a pause and I thought I'd lost her. I was looking up at the tower block she lived in. Good security. If she didn't want to see me she didn't have to. But she came back on the line. 'My time's my own,' she said. 'I'm a writer.'

I crossed my fingers. 'Glen said. How's it going?'

'Okay. I'll tell you what, I'll talk to you if you agree to answer some questions about your profession. How long have you been in it?'

'You mean the questions start now, on the phone?'

The laugh again, but a little more uncertain. 'No, I . . .'

'I've been at it a long time. I'll be happy to answer your questions.'

'Come on, then. You know where I am, I take it?'

'Yes.'

'I want you to stand back from the peephole and hold your ID up to the camera so I can be sure.'

'Okay. While I'm down here is there anything you'd like me to bring up?'

'Oh, that's so sweet of you. Why don't you surprise me.'

Women will do that. My ex-wife, Cyn, used to

say, 'Buy me something nice for lunch.' It puts you squarely on the back foot, which is why they do it. Mind you, she was always happy with what I got, however mundane. I didn't have much to go on with Birgit except what Glen had told me and how she'd sounded on the phone. I bought a bottle of top line chardonnay and a punnet of strawberries. Wine is sexy, strawberries aren't. When in doubt, sit on the fence.

I buzzed unit 50 of 85, announced myself, and the door opened. I took the lift to the tenth floor and found the door. The unit was on the west side, probably not the prime location. The camera was positioned high right, above the doorway. Juggling the wine and strawberries, I rang the bell, held my licence folder up towards the lens and tried to look strong and resolute for the peephole.

The door opened. She was small, very small, 155 centimetres tops. Silky blonde hair, straight. Olive skin. Big eyes, wide mouth, cheekbones. She wore a white singlet top and black pants, both tight. No shoes. Her finger and toenails were fire-engine red so that taking her hand was like receiving a brightly wrapped package.

'Mr Hardy, I'm so glad to meet you. And look what you've *brought*! What a sweet man.'

'Ms Hansen.' The air-conditioning was on high but her hand was warm to the touch.

'Oh, Birgit, please. Come in. Come in. The place is a mess but I'm working, you see.'

I followed her down the pale grey hallway to a pale grey room with French windows leading out to a balcony. If this was a mess my place was a junkyard. The floor was polished, the white rug was where it should be, the leather couch and chairs were precisely aligned, magazines were in their rack and books were aligned just so — hardcovers with hardcovers, paperbacks with paperbacks. I haven't known many writers but I doubted they shelved their books like that as a rule. Maybe her study was a mess. Coffee stains on the floppy disks.

She fluttered red-tipped fingers at the couch. 'Sit. It's not too early for you is it? Of course not. Private detectives have claret on their cornflakes.'

She gave a tinkling laugh and floated off to come back immediately with two glasses and a bottle opener. If I had sat I'd have been straight up again. She handed the fixings to me. Couldn't risk the nails. She plucked the clingwrap from the strawberries, used one of the long nails like an auger to remove the stem and gobbled a strawberry.

'Mm, yum. What's that movie where he says strawberries bring out the flavour of the wine except he doesn't drink?'

'*Pretty Woman*,' I said. I'd seen it with Glen back when.

'That's right. How clever. I always forget movie titles.' She watched me pour the wine and ate another strawberry. 'I remember important things though.'

'That's good,' I said. I passed her a glass and held mine out to be touched. 'To memory.'

We drank and sat, me on the couch and her on a chair, less than a metre apart. She put the strawberries on a low table to one side and when she bent forward for one the thin singlet stretched over her breasts. Her nipples were hard but I had the feeling she'd excited herself rather than had been excited.

'I liked Glen Withers,' she said. 'Dynamite lady. Are you and she an item?'

I shook my head. 'No. Colleagues.'

'Mm, well matched I'd have thought, but what do I know. All the men I think I match up with go up in smoke.'

I smiled politely. For the sake of the reading public I hoped her writing was better than this but somehow I doubted it. I drank some wine that wasn't as good as the price suggested it should have been. Birgit barely tasted hers before setting the glass aside and leaning forward to give me an even better idea of the peaks and valleys. I remembered a phrase Helen Broadway, a girlfriend from the last century, had used about another woman: 'She's not the kind of woman that other women trust.' It seemed to fit Birgit, assuming it worked in reverse. Glen had said she'd given her short shrift whereas now she appeared to have all the time in the world.

Time to test it. 'Rodney Harkness,' I said.

She shuddered. 'Slime.'

'You knew he was dead?'

'I read about it. Have they found out who did it?'

'No. That's what I'm looking into in a sort of a way.'

'I can't think why. Anyway, I'll tell you one thing.'

‘Yes?’

‘I’ll bet it was a woman.’

I was pretty sure it wasn’t; there aren’t many Myra Hindleys in the world, but it was an interesting comment. ‘Why’s that?’

‘He was poison to women. They couldn’t get enough of him and he couldn’t care less about them.’

‘Okay. What I really want to ask you about was Juliet, his sister.’

Her smooth, olive brow wrinkled but only for a split second. Didn’t want to etch wrinkles in. Great control. ‘Yes, I remember her. She’s a case in point.’

I sipped some more of the bad wine just for something to do. ‘Can you explain that?’

She almost hugged herself. ‘This is interesting, isn’t it? I mean you’re investigating and I’m a sort of a witness.’

‘Or informant.’

‘I like witness better, but, okay, that’ll do.’

I’d met people like her before. They lived in a fantasy world more or less and were astonished and delighted when their dream world and reality coincided. The trick with them was not to let reality shatter the dream.

‘Anything you can tell me about her could be very useful, Birgit.’

She ate another strawberry and a few drops of the juice spilled down onto her singlet. She didn’t notice. ‘Let’s see. I only met her once or twice. Dark, very good-looking. Younger than Rod and a lot younger than that awful Warren.

Oh, I remember now. The rumour was that the old guy wasn't really her father. You knew the old lady was Jewish.'

'No.'

'Oh, yes. Double Bay. It didn't show with Warren and Rodney but the story was that the mother had an affair with a Rabbi and Juliet was the result. Juliet looked very Jewish. Aren't you going to write this down?'

Anything to please. I pulled out my notebook and wrote a few words. Something jigged in my memory as I wrote but it slipped away immediately. 'Go on.'

'Oh, there's not that much really. Juliet turned out to be even more of a black sheep than Rodney. Although he helped her along.'

'Were they close?'

She ran her finger around the edge of her wine glass but no note sounded. 'You knew Rodney, didn't you?'

'Briefly, yes.'

'Must have been very briefly. Rodney was only close to two people — Rodney and Elvis Presley. God, did I get sick and tired of those tapes.'

'The Sun sessions,' I said.

She nodded. 'And the rest — "Jailhouse Rock" and all. I mean that's *so fifties*!'

I could easily see why the fifties wouldn't appeal to Birgit — starched petticoats and twinsets and Maidenform bras — but I was getting tired of her attitudes. 'What happened to her?'

'She was out with a couple of Rodney's friends and got killed in a car crash. He just missed being in the same car. Come to think of it, I could've been there as well, but I'd dropped him by then I'm glad to say.'

'Do you know any of the names of these people?'

'Why?'

'Well, as a writer you know how it is — lists of names. You compile lists and see if they match.'

'Of course. Wow, this is really useful for me.'

'Names?'

The brow wrinkled again and held the grooves a fraction longer. 'Only one comes to mind. Her boyfriend at the time. He was somebody Mitchell. No, Mitchell somebody. Mitchell Sexton, that's it. He wasn't in the car. It's a funny name, isn't it. Sexton suggests church and then there's sex in it. He was waiting for her to arrive at his place. It was very sad. Her family didn't like him. He was a policeman. Not good enough, you see. Were you ever a policeman, Cliff? Most private detectives were, I believe.'

I wasn't listening to her. Sexton — the name was on the list of Lucille's lovers. Things were clicking into place and I was hearing the clicks.

25

It took me a while to get clear of Birgit Hansen and I promised to stay in touch with her and let her know how things turned out — promises I had no intention of keeping. As soon as I was out of the building I hauled out my notebook and looked up the number for Brett Hughes, the crippled policeman. I hadn't mentioned Hughes to the police, perhaps because I'd been thrown off balance by his disability and hadn't taken any notes during our interview. All I had was the scrawled phone number and my eye had travelled right over it when I'd been reviewing the notes.

I used the mobile now, on the assumption that the chances of catching disabled people at home are better than average. Hughes was Mr Efficiency; he recited the number and then gave his name.

'This is Cliff Hardy, Mr Hughes, remember me?'

'Yeah, sure. And I see you lost your man.'

'That's right. How're things with you?'

'Okay. What can I do for you?'

'Well, I'm still on it. I've got another client. Sort of insurance matter.'

'Uh, yeah? Well?'

Not a good start. I didn't blame him. Policing is a lousy job for the most part, and the thought of those others of us who work the same street for money doesn't sit easily with honest cops. I was in tricky territory, trying to tease out information about a possibly still serving police officer from someone who wasn't stupid and was probably still loyal to the service. I thought my chances of getting under his guard were slim. Best to come clean.

'I think you can help me but I want to be straight with you. It might involve another policeman. I think I should fill you in properly and then see if you want to help me.'

The silence was long and deep. I could imagine him sitting there in his wheelchair with all that upper body strength trapped and anchored, but I couldn't even guess at what would be in his mind. I heard him expel a deep breath. 'I appreciate that, Hardy. Okay, I'm on my way to the gym — Lakemba Fitness Centre, Haldon Street, near where we had coffee.'

'I'll find it,' I said. 'I could do with a workout myself. Visitors welcome?'

But he'd rung off.

The further west I went the hotter the day became. By the time I got to Lakemba the temperature had to be pushing 30 degrees and the Muslim women's robes and veils started to make some sense. I trawled along looking for the gym and prepared to be frustrated because, in my experience, such places in residential areas tend to be tucked away, half-hidden by struggling used car yards and small drive-in shopping centres. The Lakemba Sports and Fitness Centre conformed to the pattern. It was the poor relation beside a supermarket, a computer supplies store and a medical complex grouped around a lumpy bitumen parking area where the white lines had been almost obliterated by oil stains.

I hauled my gym bag out of the boot and approached the entrance to the centre. A white Honda Civic stood in one of the handicapped parking spots and I could see the tracks of the wheelchair leading up the ramp to the front of the building as I took the steps. A young Asian woman who wouldn't have weighed sixty kilos sat behind the reception desk doing paperwork.

'Yes, sir?'

'I'm meeting someone here, Brett Hughes. But I'd also like to have a workout.'

'You have a gym membership in the city?'

'Yes, at Leichhardt.' I found the card in my wallet.

'Welcome to Lakemba. Ten dollars, please.'

I changed and went through to the weights room where a very mixed bag of humanity was working out — men and women of all shapes and sizes and ethnic origins. I saw Hughes moving massive weights at a seated bench press. He completed his set, looked up and saw me and went back to work. I did fifteen minutes on the treadmill and then wandered around the unfamiliar location, picking out the machines I was accustomed to and doing my usual, unadventurous sets.

After a session of pull-downs I ended up near Hughes, who was doing curls with free weights somewhere in the 50 kilo range. His wheelchair was parked in the corner of the room.

'How're you doing?' I said when he'd finished his set.

He was sweating freely and he reached for his towel. 'Getting there,' he said. 'I can haul myself around from machine to machine in here. I'll be through in ten minutes.'

'The coffee place?'

He picked up a weight that would've broken my wrist if I'd tried to lift it from the rack. 'Fuck that, I'm due a beer. Pub on the corner.'

I did another ten minutes on the treadmill set to 8 with an incline of 5. Trotting. Then I went to the pub. It was an old one re-vamped, with poker machines and a screen flashing keno numbers.

Hughes wheeled himself into the bar, greeted a few regulars and shook my hand. 'Mine's a schooner of New,' he said.

Sounded good. I made it two and took the drinks over to the table where he'd installed himself with a pencil and a keno ticket. He filled in the ticket and one of the drinkers took it across to the counter for him.

'Good luck,' I said.

'Don't strain yourself in the gym, do you?'

'I'm toning.'

'Bullshit.' He took a drink and checked his ticket against the screen. 'Not quite. Okay, Hardy, what's on your mind?'

'Before we get to it, what's your take on the

police service these days? Are you well disposed, or what?'

He picked at one of the calluses on his left hand. 'I don't know that I've got an attitude to it overall. They're treating me right over the disability, no worries there. I'd say I see it as a collection of individuals. That's a bad thing.'

'Meaning?'

'You should be able to see it as a whole and support it as a whole but you can't. There's good and bad in it, very good and very bad. Between you and me, I'm writing a book on the subject.'

Another writer. What he'd said was encouraging, though, particularly that he'd confided in me. 'Won't you need some sort of clearance to publish a book?'

He shrugged. 'If I decide to go that way. Come on, Hardy, stop beating around the bush.'

'Right. Take your mind back to when you were in the station and you'd put Rodney Harkness in the cells after he'd raved on about what he'd done.'

Hughes finished his schooner. 'If you're going to ask me who was there it's no good. I've tried to remember and it's too long ago with too much fucking happening in between.'

'Another drink?'

'No. I just have the one.'

'All right. I understand what you're saying. I suppose I'd be surprised if you could remember a detail like that. How about I try a name on you?'

'Go.'

'Mitchell Sexton.'

He looked up and for a minute I thought he

was checking his keno result again but he had that long stare running down the corridor of memory. 'Jesus Christ,' he said. 'Sexy Sexton. Yeah, he was there that night. I remember now. And I told him what Harkness had said.'

'What did he say?'

'I can't remember. Not much or maybe nothing. He certainly never reported on it and then Harkness was off the books as it were. Some kind of top brass intervention there. I didn't think any more about it. What's going on?'

I told him that Sexton had been involved with Rodney Harkness's sister and then had been Harkness's wife's lover, one of them. 'If Sexton blamed Harkness for the sister's death and then heard him confessing to his wife's murder he might well have reason to kill him.'

'Plus if influence got him tucked away in a comfortable funny farm.'

'Yeah. What can you tell me about Sexton?'

'Only that he was an obnoxious prick. Full of himself. Thought everything he said and did was interesting when mostly it wasn't, or not nearly as interesting as he reckoned.'

'I know the type,' I said. 'I need another drink to work on this. You sure?'

Hughes shrugged. 'I'd say it's a two-drink problem all right.'

I brought the drinks back. Hughes tore up his keno ticket and piled the pieces in the ashtray. 'Any thoughts?'

'Do you happen to know whether he was a sharpshooter?'

'Dunno. Sorry.'

'Likely to go off the rails over something like this?'

'Hard to say. He was always on the make. Ambitious, like. He was honest as far as I know, but a chip-on-the-shoulder type. I mean, he didn't come from money or anything. Not many of us do . . . did. I'd say he'd be a bit out of his depth with people like Harkness. Resentful if they got the better of him, but a nutter . . . a killer, I don't know.'

I drank and thought aloud. 'He'd have to keep it festering for seven years, so I guess it'd depend how things went for him after Harkness got locked away. You don't know whether he's still on the force?'

'In the service you mean.'

'Whatever.'

'No, I don't know. Wouldn't be hard to find out. You've got the contacts — Frank Parker, Glen Withers . . .'

'I suppose.'

'So what's the problem?'

'I'd said I'd be straight with you. Investigating a copper, whether serving or not, isn't my idea of fun. Plus I don't know where you stand.'

'Me?'

'Suppose I say I'm going to look into him, watch him, talk to his neighbours, root through his rubbish bin, what would your attitude be?'

He finished his beer and pushed the glass firmly aside. 'You don't think Harkness killed his wife, do you?'

'A psychiatrist I respect says he didn't.'

'I heard a whisper he didn't die easy.'

'He was tortured.'

'I've got no time for shit like that. Go for it, Hardy. I'm out, but I'll give you a bit of advice. Cover your arse — talk it over with Parker or with someone from Internal Affairs or the fucking Ombudsman. You're right, going up against a policeman isn't easy.'

I thanked him. We shook hands and I walked beside him as he wheeled himself out of the pub.

I had a lot to think about and I found myself driving home to do the thinking. If there were things waiting for me in the office they could wait. The Sexton lead felt solid but I knew I'd need evidence. I wondered if Glen had had the rifle bullet examined before she took off with Rod. To do anything with that I'd need to find the rifle. Was Sexton a shooter? For that matter, was he still a policeman and where did he live? Rodney Harkness had been burnt with cigarettes but no butts had been found at the site. Therefore no DNA. Did that indicate a policeman's professionalism or just commonsense caution? He'd been executed with a pistol shot. Did the police have the bullet? They hadn't told me and wouldn't.

It was early in the afternoon when I reached home and I wanted to talk things over with Jerry but it wasn't the time to ring her; heavy consultation time. I collected the mail and went inside to make a sandwich and write a summary of the interview with Brett Hughes and where things now stood. For no good reason I had a mental image of what it'd be like to be tortured with a cigarette and mutilated with bolt cutters. It put me off the sandwich. I threw it in the bin and sat down with my notebook. I noticed that the light on the answering machine was blinking and as I reached to touch the button my mobile rang. Confused, I paused my finger above the machine and answered the mobile.

'Hardy? This is Kevin Sherrin. I want to know what you're fucking playing at. I know you saw Glen today. I hope you're happy. She's in the Prince of Wales. She tried to kill herself.'

26

I went straight to the hospital and met up with Sherrin. He was thumbing through magazines in a waiting room on the ward where Glen was being held for observation. Although I knew he had no liking for me, the relief at having something to kick against showed on his face almost like a welcome.

'How is she?' I asked.

'Sick, but she'll recover. They say I can see her in a while when they're sure her system's clean. They're going to keep her overnight at least.'

'What happened?'

He threw the magazine down. 'That's what I should fucking-well ask you. I was worried about her. She seemed to be better for a while with the AA meetings and all and then she went down again. So I got home as early as I could. I'm still on this fucking course. She was on the bed and barely breathing. There were notes for both of us, you and me.'

He'd got to his feet when I'd come in and now was shaking, partly from anger, partly from distress, partly from exhaustion. The waiting room was small and hot but we had it to ourselves. I felt very sorry for him. I've been around suicides and attempted suicides and the survivors quite a few times and the dynamics are complicated. When notes are left, at the very least the recipient expects to be the focus of attention. Sharing the receipt of the intended suicide's last message isn't in the script. Sherrin was confused as much as he was hurt and angry and it wasn't hard to encourage him to sit down and talk.

'She . . . just told me she was sorry and that she knew I loved her and it wasn't enough for her to go on with. I read your note as well.'

I nodded. I would've done the same.

'It was all about feeling responsible for what happened to Harkness. She said that seeing you had brought it all home to her and she couldn't handle it.'

He started to sob. 'Fuck you, Hardy, with your push and shove and never give up. Fuck you!'

There was nothing I could say. I sat and let the moment pass. Eventually he wiped his eyes. 'She told you to find out who killed Harkness. Fat chance.'

I let that go as well. When he seemed to have calmed down a bit I said, 'You must've moved bloody quickly.'

'Huh. Yeah, well, we're trained, aren't we. I had the ambulance there in minutes. She'd gone out and bought a bottle of Scotch to take the pills with. In a way that saved her life.'

'How?'

'She was still struggling against the booze even when she was giving up on life. She didn't ingest enough alcohol to make the pills kick in properly. She's tough, Glen. Her body didn't want to die.'

'Mr Sherrin. You can see your wife now.'

A nurse had appeared at the doorway. Sherrin got up and walked away after her without giving me another look. I sat and thought about him and Glen and Harkness and Jerry and me. About winners and losers and everyone in between. So far, Rodney St John was the biggest loser but I didn't see why any of the rest of us had to fall into the same group.

Sherrin had left the jacket of his suit over a chair in the waiting room so I knew he'd be back. While I sat there I planned what I could say to him. I was still pushing and shoving, still not giving up.

About ten minutes later he walked in and reached for his jacket. He was in that space where other people don't matter and he was scarcely aware of me until I handed him the coat.

'Don't ask,' he said.

'I won't, but I have to talk to you and you have to listen for your sake and for Glen's.'

We went to a pub in Randwick and I laid it all on the line for Sherrin. Despite his antagonism towards me and the pressure he was under trying to deal with Glen, the policeman in him came to the fore and he listened and took in what I was saying. We were drinking whisky, pacing ourselves, heavy on the water. Two plates of potato wedges with sour cream. The pub was fairly quiet but there was enough background noise for us to speak in normal voices.

'That's bloody thin,' Sherrin said when I'd finished and dealt with the few questions he'd posed.

'I know. But there's something in it. It just needs bolstering, like finding Sexton's rifle . . .'

'If he's got one.'

'And his pistol.'

'Likewise. At least I know where that bullet you gave Glen is. I can get it tested.'

'And you can find out what we need to know about Sexton.'

'If I agree to help you.'

I didn't say, *Glen needs this to be closed.* I didn't have to. I wolfed down a couple of the potato chunks. Sherrin seemed uninterested in the food but he played with his drink while he thought it all over. I didn't rush him. I was tired at the end of a long day. I wanted to talk to Jerry.

Sherrin surprised me then. 'What does your psychiatrist girlfriend think?' he said.

'This all came together today. I haven't had a chance to talk to her.'

'This is the first drink I've had since I came up to Broken Beach and collected Glen. Mind you, I had a few on board then.'

I'd noticed that he'd lost weight since the last time I'd talked to him. 'Must be tough.'

He nodded. 'Funny you should bring this to me just now. I'm on a course that'll give me a promotion into Internal Affairs if I do all right. They're a hard-drinking mob, trying to prove they're still the boyos. They think I'm a wuss.'

'They might think a bit different if this works out.'

He drained his drink and got up to get more. I wasn't going to stop him. I'd get a taxi home if need be. He went off chewing on a couple of wedges. When he came back he said, '*If* I do it, it'll be for Glen's sake, not mine and not yours.'

'Understood.'

'Did Glen say anything about me when you saw her this morning?'

'Only that she was giving you a hard time.'

'Tell me this — have you still got any intentions towards her?'

I shook my head. 'Other inclinations.'

'Right. Well, I reckon I ought to back off a bit.' He picked up a couple of wedges, dipped them in the sour cream and ate them. Then he had a couple more. The food seemed to aid his resolution. 'Tell you what I'll do. I'll go back to my place tonight and go in as normal tomorrow. I'll leave you to get Glen home and settled and you can tell her what we're doing.'

'You're saying you're in?'

'I am. Yes. We've got computer time tomorrow. I'll see what I can dig up and get back to you, say by mid-afternoon. Let's see how Glen takes to it all. If she's okay and we've got anything to work on we can pick it up from there. Sort of keep her in the loop. See if it works. If she's still too fragile, I don't know. We'll have to think again.'

It was a good result, holding to his desired line

and potentially getting me what I wanted, and I agreed to it in every detail, although I asked him to phone the hospital and give his authority for me to stand in for him. He agreed. 'It's all bullshit anyway,' he said. 'I'm not really her husband. Not any more.'

This time we shook hands.

I'd had four Scotches and was tossing up whether to get a taxi as I stood by my car with the keys in my hand. 'Be smart,' I said aloud. 'You have to be over here tomorrow morning anyway.' A few passers-by looked at me.

My mobile rang and I answered it, glad to be able to put the decision off. It was Jerry and I realised that I'd forgotten to ring her with all that had been going on.

'Coming over?'

'Can't,' I said. 'I . . .'

'Are you pissed?'

'I've had a couple but I'm okay.'

'Get a cab.'

I unlocked the car and sat in the passenger seat. I explained what had happened and how I'd agreed to collect Glen the following morning and why. The silence wasn't golden.

'Sounds to me like she needs professional help.'

'I'm sure you're right, but I have to do this. I have to cooperate with Sherrin and . . .'

'I'm beginning to wish . . . no, I *do* wish I hadn't agreed to back you on this. Turn it over to the police, Cliff.'

'We haven't got enough.'

'Right. And how're you going to get more? Break into his house? Can't you see a few problems with that? The two of you are fumbling around on account of this woman. For a smart and experienced man you're not thinking clearly.'

'You might be right.'

'Stop patronising me. If I'm right, if you *see* that that that I'm right, act accordingly.'

It was the wrong tack for her to take with me after the events of the day and when I had some alcohol on board. Enough to make me feel right and clever. I probably sounded more brusque than I meant to. 'I'm going to do it this way.'

'Okay,' she said and hung up.

I sat there with the phone in my hand, feeling empty and let down. The booze buzz died rapidly away leaving me sour and not clever at all. The positives got replaced by negatives. *Do psychiatrists feel jealousy? Aren't they above that?* I shoved across to the driver's seat, started up and drove home.

I was really in no condition to drive, not drunk but probably over the limit and tired, dispirited and underfed with it. Low blood sugar. I drove on auto and got a couple of adrenalin jolts at near misses that helped to keep me alert enough to make it back to Glebe. I don't know what it is but there's something that comforts me about driving down Glebe Point Road. It's not just going home, because that has many sorts of associations, not all of them good. It's something to do with the honest, solid old buildings on both sides of the road, the water at the bottom, the expanse of the park.

Buildings, water, trees — I was thinking about them, how they were more dependable than people, as I turned into my street and realised that the alcohol was still working in me.

I parked and went inside and had a decision to make. The drinker's decision. To have some more and keep this edge I was feeling, this almost philosophical acceptance of things as they were. It's one of the benefits of drinking, but it doesn't usually lead anywhere. Or sober up and think things through — Glen, Sherrin, Jerry — all that. I was still tossing up about it when the phone rang.

I snatched it up. 'Jerry?'

'Hardy? This is Lance Matthiesson. I've been leaving messages.'

The light was blinking. 'Matthiesson? Yeah, okay. What?'

'Are you all right?'

'I'm tired. Big day.'

'Aren't they all? Thing is, we need you to identify a body. The good news is he's in the Glebe morgue. Just down the way from you.'

'Very funny,' I said. 'Who?'

'That's not the way it plays. You be there at 7.30 tomorrow morning.'

My head was spinning, trying to process the information, and I still hadn't resolved the alcohol question. 'What's wrong with now? Tonight?'

'Fuck you. Seven-thirty a.m. Sharp!'

27

The morgue is in Arundel Street, across Ross Street, where it trundles down to a dead end just short of Parramatta Road. The building is flat to the footpath, a plum-coloured brick box with big roller doors for the ambulances. The only attractive thing about it is the painted sign above the entrance. It reads 'Forensic Medicine' and has a set of scales and an open book. Nice touch. There's a pleasant set of single-storey sandstone terraces across the street, but the building's reflecting windows seem to say once you're in, you're in.

'In here.'

'I know where to go.'

Matthiesson shepherded me into the soulless space, looking less comfortable than I was, even though he was far from a first-timer. I'd laid off the drink but my sleep had been fitful with thoughts of Glen and Jerry and irritation at Matthiesson's caginess in the mix. We went through the dance with the female attendant who peeled back the plastic cover and stepped away.

He looked younger in death than he had in life

and oddly healthier. There were no wounds on his head and his features were relaxed.

'Craig,' I said. 'How?'

The attendant covered him and Matthiesson and I walked away. I was breathing shallowly the way you do, as if sucking in too much of the air in that place would do you harm.

'Overdose,' Matthiesson said. 'Hot shot almost certainly. Signs of a struggle, pressure on the carotid.'

We left the building and walked around the corner and into Parramatta Road where Matthiesson was parked. The dirty air and noisy traffic were somehow comforting. 'You found my card on him,' I said.

'No. We printed him. Got a match with the doorlock and the keys under the brick. You told us about paying someone to fix the lock.'

'Are you telling me there was no one else to identify him?'

'That's right. He was found in a skip at a building site in Bondi. Some change in his pockets. That's all. No room key, no nothing. Probably wearing all the clothes he owned. Lighter, two cigarettes. Looks like he was on the streets. Who kills a harmless junkie unless he knows or sees something he shouldn't? Give me your thoughts, Hardy.'

'You're sure about the hot shot?'

'Pretty sure. Blood test says high quality heroin in quantity. He would have been a skin popper, a sniffer and a smoker more than a mainliner, and he wouldn't have had the money for stuff like that.

The autopsy'll tell us more. Are you examining your conscience?'

'I asked him to ring me if he saw the guy who broke into the flat again. I didn't tell him to do any more than that.'

'You gave him money. You know what they're like. Give them a smell . . .'

'Okay. He saw him again. Got too close and was spotted. Easy after that for the killer, especially if he's a policeman.'

'Got any more on that?'

That was the question. What was the answer? I had Sherrin on the job but possibly too emotionally involved to be reliable. Jerry urging me to turn the whole matter over to the police and now only tenuously available as a protective client. And Matthiesson offside, potentially hostile, no doubt looking for a result himself. The cards were stacked against the course Sherrin and I had set ourselves.

'No,' I said. 'Nothing.' I looked at my watch. 'I have to be somewhere. It's tough about the kid, but he didn't have a bright future anyway.'

Matthiesson turned away. 'You're a bastard, Hardy.'

'I've heard that before.'

He stalked off in his nice suit towards his air-conditioned car and I didn't feel quite as much like a bastard as he thought I should. What I was feeling was something else altogether. Suppose Craig didn't have a place to lay his head and was wearing all the clothes he owned? Suppose the killer of Rodney Harkness had taken him out?

Suppose all that — where was my card, the one I'd given Craig before I set off for the Central Coast at what now seemed like a long time ago? The one he'd buttoned so carefully into his shirt pocket. Did the killer have it? Maybe. Did Craig lose it or throw it away? Maybe.

I'd skipped breakfast, not sure what Matthiesson would have in store for me. Now, I was hungry the minute I was out of the morgue. I wandered down to the first of the coffee shops in Glebe Point Road and ordered coffee and raisin toast. The day had dawned grey and was getting greyer around the edges. It was still warm for so early and there was a threat or promise of rain, depending on whether you were playing golf or growing roses. Personally, I didn't care one way or the other. As I ate I realised that I was watching everyone who came into the place and the people who were eating out on the street. The passers-by. Normally, I'd have eaten outside myself, but not today. It was getting to me.

A kid with a batch of newspapers came in and I bought the morning paper, ran my eye over the headlines, flicked to the editorial page and read the leader and a couple of letters and then settled into the sports section. Kostya Tszyu was scheduled to meet someone I'd never heard of to defend his unified super-lightweight title. I remembered seeing him fight at the Parramatta football stadium a few years back and hearing the fans yelling, 'Zoo, Zoo. Zoo' and thinking Australia isn't such a bad place when it can take a little Russian with a pigtail to its heart. But that was before the *Tampa* and the World Trade Center and all the other political horrors. I read through the news where everything in the sports I was interested in — boxing, tennis, athletics — was normal. But nothing felt normal about what I was doing and the people I was doing it with and for.

A call to the hospital told me that I could collect Ms Withers at 10.30 a.m., and that Superintendent Sherrin had arranged for me to park in the staff car park near the entrance. I was in a state of high confusion. If Rod's killer was a cop he could've ID'd me from the car registration when I'd collected Rod but deemed me to be just a hireling. That'd change if the card I'd given Craig had come into his hands. If he had me tagged and was interested, was it wise for me to be transporting Glen? Did the killer have any reason to feel insecure? If he'd killed Craig because of his association with me, he must have some qualms. If he knew Glen was investigating Harkness — easy enough for a cop to find out because she'd worked through Missing Persons — he could conclude that she'd put things together, like the lovers of Juliet Harkness and Lucille Hammond. Too many assumptions, I decided. I drove to Randwick and parked inside the hospital grounds, glad I didn't have to contend with patients, visitors and students from the University of New South Wales whose cars were filling the available spaces outside.

I went to the administration block and presented my ID. Despite deciding to behave as if we had a clear run I found myself examining other people in the waiting room. I shook my head and told myself I was paranoid. Clock a well-built man in suit with a groomed moustache and there's something to think about. Otherwise, forget it.

Glen came through a perspex door into the reception area. She was wearing a dark dress and medium heels. She had makeup on and her hair had been washed and brushed into shape. She had a gold chain around her neck and wore earrings, something I'd never seen her do before. She gave me a smile and a small wave and I approached the clerk, a young Asian guy, handling the exiting patients with her.

'Hi,' she said as she handed over her papers. 'You're supposed to present your ID.'

I nodded, passed my driver's licence to the clerk and tried not to look as if I was checking her over. But I was. Under the makeup she was pale and her quick smile looked painted on. Still, she was moving with something like her usual athletic grace and she gave the plastic bag she was carrying a jaunty swing.

'Thank you, Ms Withers, Mr Hardy,' the clerk said after he tapped some keys and handed Glen a printout sheet and returned my licence.

'Thank *you*,' Glen said and her voice was a little louder than it needed to be.

I took her arm and felt her flinch and then relax as if she was resigning herself to something unpleasant. We walked out of the hospital into the grey, windy day and I wished it could have been bright and sunny for her to welcome her back to the land of the living.

'Shitty day,' she said.

'Could be worse. Could be raining.'

Just as I spoke a couple of drops fell and then a few more and the wind dropped and the rain started to fall just a little harder as if it was picking up the beat. We both laughed and the dark mood was broken. I pointed to the car park.

'Kevin got me a spot. Lucky.'

'That'd be right,' Glen said. 'The man thinks of everything.'

We were only slightly wet when we got to the car. Glen slung her plastic bag over the back and settled into the battered vinyl bench seat. 'Why don't you get rid of this old bomb?'

'It goes.'

She laughed. 'And it leaks.' A drop of moisture appeared on the dashboard in front of her and she prodded it with a painted fingernail. Another first for Glen in my experience — painted nails. The rain hammered on the roof and we sat there for a few minutes by unspoken mutual consent listening to the sound and watching the world getting hosed down.

'You hate the rain, don't you, Cliff?'

'I used to. As I get older I'm coming to accept it.'

Her head jerked and she was looking directly at me. 'Dumb thing to do, wasn't it?'

'Desperate, anyway.'

She relaxed. 'Yeah. I couldn't see any reason to

make it to tomorrow because I thought tomorrow'd be worse than today and the day after that'd be worse still.'

'And now?'

'I think that's being a bit over-dramatic, taking myself too seriously. I mean, what do I really matter in the scheme of things? It's a big world, lots going on. Best to hang around and watch it. What d'you reckon?'

I started the car and was relieved to hear it fire up. No water in the distributor. Not yet. 'It sounds like a workable position. Might need a bit of shoring up here and there.'

'Mm. In a way I envy women with kids. I've known a few who'd have offed themselves long ago if it wasn't for the kids. I don't know what keeps fucked-up blokes afloat.'

I negotiated my way out of the car park, hoping the wipers would maintain their rhythm. 'Stubbornness mostly,' I said. 'Fear of one kind or another. Do you want to go straight home or what?'

I pulled out onto the street and joined the line of cautious traffic. She sat quite still, staring through the windscreen and it was some time before she spoke. 'Kevin said you've got a lead on who killed Rodney.'

'Could be.'

'Can I come back to your place?'

'Not a good idea, Glen.'

'Okay. Your girlfriend. I understand. Right. Home then to my groovy Paddington pad.' She dropped her head and began to weep quietly.

Glen pulled herself together with an effort when we got to her house. She made coffee, checked her mail, did some tidying and cleaning, kept busy. I chatted to her, helped out here and there and tried not to think about Rod Harkness or Kevin Sherrin or Mitchell Sexton. I noticed that Glen kept glancing at her watch. We listened to the ABC news at noon and then left 'The World Today' on, turned down low.

'That's a relief,' Glen said.

'What is?'

'Getting past midday without a drink. It's downhill all the way now till six o'clock. Then it hits hard again.'

'You shouldn't wear a watch. Should turn the clocks to the wall.'

She laughed. 'Don't worry. An alkie knows exactly what time it is, watch or no watch.' She found a bottle of mineral water in the fridge and poured two glasses. Put not quite stale buns on a plate with some cheese and sliced tomatoes, and told me to sit down at the tiny kitchen table. 'Okay, Cliff,' she said. 'Tell me what the fuck you and Kevin are up to.'

I looked at her astonished. 'He hasn't told you?'

'I'm too fragile to be *told* anything, aren't I?' She parodied Sherrin's bass voice: '"Don't worry, love. I've asked Hardy to look after you tomorrow . . ." Bullshit!'

To give myself time to think, I drank some mineral water, slicked open a bun and put cheese and tomato in it.

'If you start eating that I'll throw this knife at you.'

'Okay. He's overprotective but he's actually got your best interests at heart. I'm sure of it.'

'Fuckin' tell me.'

So I told her in detail, leaving nothing out. She listened without interrupting, except to express surprise at the connection between Sexton and the two women. It took a while and by the time I'd finished I'd drunk the mineral water and was hungry so I took a bite out of the bun.

'Why?' she said.

I had to talk around the food. 'He thinks you feel guilty about what happened to Harkness. If we can nail the killer it might help.'

She snorted. 'That's pretty crude psychology. What does your girlfriend think about that?'

I'd managed not to think about Jerry and now I had to. I swallowed and lost my appetite. 'She's pissed off. Told me to give it all to the police. Hung up on me last time we spoke.'

'Sensible woman. Poor Cliff.'

'Poor Rod. Poor Craig, maybe.'

Glen played with her glass and prodded at the food with the knife she'd threatened to throw. 'I've never heard of this Sexton, so he obviously hasn't got to the top. Still, he could be someone very senior somewhere. It's a big organisation. You should've asked Parker about him.'

'Kevin's looking into it, as I said. He's got the facilities.'

'Kevin isn't subtle, Cliff. He's very likely to advertise what he's doing. What then?'

I shrugged. 'I don't know. Tell you this, though. It was you turning up Sexton's name in connection with the wife that gave us the lead. I mean when it cross-referenced with the sister's lover.'

Neither of us was going to eat the food. She dumped it in the kitchen tidy and stacked the plates. 'Big deal,' she said. 'Call Parker. I'm going to have a nap.'

She left the kitchen and I heard one of the doors off the passage close firmly. I got up and went to the back of the house and sat in an easy chair. The light was dim and the rain on the tin roof was steady. I took out my mobile and thought about calling Frank. Hughes had advised it and so had Glen. A good move, no doubt. Then I thought about calling Jerry. Bad time. She'd either be with a client or taking a break. And what would I say? Nothing had changed. I didn't call her either. The glassed-in back room was warm and the rain on the roof was lulling. So was the low murmur of radio voices. My head fell back and I dropped off into a deep, dreamless sleep.

I jerked awake to a quieter world. The rain had stopped and a beam of light had penetrated the glass and bounced back at me from a glass-topped table. My dry mouth told me I'd been asleep for more than a few minutes. My watch told me it was a bit over an hour.

'Glen?'

I hauled myself out of the chair and went down the passage. The bedroom door was open and I blundered in. The pillow held the imprint of her head but she wasn't there.

28

The space between Glen's house and the street was enough to sit in, just. I took a look there without optimism. I prowled back through the house trying to get an idea of where she might have gone. Her handbag was missing and there were coats and jackets thrown over a chair in the bedroom suggesting she'd taken a coat. The other room was a study cum office. No computer. At least that was encouraging; she wasn't likely to have taken her computer if she'd gone off to drink, unless she intended to hock it and I couldn't see that. I pressed the redial button on the phone, but the last call had been to the hospital, obviously made by Sherrin.

I cursed myself for falling asleep and rang the contact number Sherrin had given me. He wasn't available and I left the message for him to ring back urgently. I paced up and down by the phone, heated coffee in the microwave, drank it and felt a deep need for something stronger. I opened cupboards and thought about all the likely hiding places. My mother had been ordered off the grog many times in her life and had managed dry spells from time to time. But she always had a back-up bottle somewhere and I wondered if Glen was the same. Eventually I found it in one of my mother's old hidey-holes — a bottle of Hennessy brandy inside a knee-high boot with several pairs of tights stuffed down on top of it.

I took it back to the kitchen, heated more coffee and spiked it strongly. I'd taken one tongue-scorching drink when the phone rang.

'Hardy? Bit eager aren't you?'

'No, Glen's gone.'

'Fuck. How?'

'Does it matter? She's skipped. I think she's taken a coat and she's got her handbag and computer. Any ideas?'

'Just that you've fucked up.'

'Doesn't help. She seemed pretty steady. I told her everything — about Sexton and all.'

'Oh, brilliant.'

'Listen, if you treat her like a wreck she'll behave like one.'

'Jesus, Hardy. What I'd like to do to you. Okay, okay, let me think. You say she's taken her laptop?'

'If it was in the study, yes.'

'And you told her about Sexton and the two women and him being a policeman?'

'Right.'

'Well, I know what she's doing. Pretty much what I did. She's holed up somewhere with a phone connection. Hacking into files trying to locate the bastard. If I can do it, she can.'

The spiked coffee had cooled and I had another long drink. I felt I was losing my grip on everything and all of us were heading for something bad. I wasn't sure that the brandy would help but I gave it another try. 'And have you found him?'

There was an ominous silence at the other end and I could almost hear Sherrin's thought processes ticking over antagonistically. I couldn't blame him. 'Hardy,' he said. 'I'm not sure I want you in on this any more.'

I didn't say anything.

'Fuck it. I need to know something only you can tell me.'

His voice was a strained, thin version of its usual rich tone. The stress was eating him alive, but I had to take advantage of any edge I had, although I had no idea what it might be. 'If you've located Sexton and can get to him I want to be in on it whatever happens.'

'I've got him.'

'Yes?'

'He's a DI at North Manly. Gun club president. Worked drugs for years. Lives at Seaforth. I've got the address and the phone number.'

'Give them to me now and I'll tell you what you want to know.' *Whatever the hell it is,* I thought.

'You're a bastard, Hardy.'

'I know,' I said.

He rattled off the address and phone number and I scribbled them down on the phone table notepad. 'Okay. Shoot.'

His laugh was a short bark. 'Appropriate, that. Glen's got a Beretta. She keeps it in a drawer in the desk in the study. Go and look. Tell me it's still there.'

I'd already looked in the desk drawers in my hunt for the booze but I didn't need to tell Sherrin that. I put the phone down and drank some more coffee. After about the right time lapse I picked up the receiver.

'No gun,' I said.

'Shit. This is crazy. She's making a run at him herself.'

'How hard was it for you to come up with the information? How long will it take her?'

'Hard to say. It took me a while. But I guess she knows her way around those files and knows what to do if she gets stuck. It's not super-secure information.'

'She was worried that you might advertise your interest in Sexton. How likely's that for either of you?'

He was too upset to be insulted. 'Not likely.'

'Have you got any idea where she might go to do that kind of work? A friend? A motel?'

'Fuck. You'd be more likely to know that sort of thing than me. Maybe she went to your place. Maybe she's still got a key.'

'I don't think so. We have to assume she's gone after him. North Manly or Seaforth. You're official. You take Manly, I'll take his house. Maybe we can stop her.'

'I don't know . . .' Indecisiveness was in every syllable. 'I should report it officially. Get help.'

'There's no time,' I said. 'Think how long that'd take. Reckon you could explain it and get things moving inside an hour?'

'No. You're right. I'm on my way. Give me your

mobile number again. Christ, I hope we're in time.'

I gave him the mobile number, checked that I still had his card, swilled the rest of the coffee, grabbed the brandy and bolted. During the drive I was thinking that what could be shaping up was the worst of situations — one dangerous person confronted with another who was desperate and unstable. An explosive mixture. I rang the Seaforth house as I drove but got no answer. I assumed Sherrin was ringing the station at North Manly. Tougher assignment. I should have told him she hadn't gone for the brandy. Given him something.

The bleak day hadn't improved but it hadn't got worse; visibility was poor and the road surface was slick. The drivers were the usual mixture of good, bad and insane, making progress slow. We inched across the Spit Bridge where a kind of mist hung over the road and the water. Mid-afternoon, but the light was dropping as darker clouds moved in from the east. I located Sexton's street in the *Gregory's* and turned into it thinking how chaotic and improvised all this was. Did Sexton have a family? How had Glen been travelling? I realised I was in the wrong street, similar name, when the mobile rang.

'Hardy? They tell me DI Sexton left the station a short time ago in the company of a woman. Where the fuck are you?'

'Almost there. Anything else?'

'No. Get there!'

I re-checked the directory and found the street.

I'd been in the Court not the Avenue. I skidded around the corners as the rain fell heavily and the harbour mist rolled in. I got to the right street, entered it and saw a car pull into a driveway halfway along, about where the right number would be. I gunned the motor and reached the house in time to see a tall man escort a woman in a light coat up the steps and into the house.

The adrenalin was pumping but I forced myself to drive past and stop. Not a bull-at-a-gate time. I tried to recreate the scene in my mind. I'd only glimpsed them through some shrubbery, but the body language had been clear enough — the man forceful, aggressive, the woman, resistant, impelled. The glimpse had been enough to confirm that Sexton answered Craig's description of the man who'd broken into the Bondi flat, if confirmation was needed. It wasn't hard to guess what had happened. Glen had made a head-on run at Sexton and he'd come out on top. Now she was under the control of a torturer and murderer. Great work, Hardy. Great work, Sherrin.

I parked across the street and two houses back and surveyed the set-up. Fashionable middle-class neighbourhood, wide blocks, bungalows, deep-fronted gardens, two-car garages, boats, TV satellite dishes. A secure and comfortable place, suddenly not so secure and comfortable. Sherrin's Pulsar turned into the street at speed. He slowed down when he saw me, U-turned and stopped a car length behind me. His cop instincts were intact. He closed the door of his car quietly, took in the numbers of the houses and walked up to my car on the passenger side. I wound down the window.

'I was a second too late,' I said. 'Saw them go in.'

The rain was light now but persistent. He ignored it.

'Was she all right?'

'She was walking.'

He opened the door and sat with his upper body inside the car and his legs and feet in the rain. His usual high colour had paled and with his thin hair damp and flat on his head he looked older and harder. He unshipped his mobile phone.

'What're you doing?'

'You'll see. I'm in charge of this, Hardy. You do what I say.'

His voice was firmer and his manner more confident than I'd ever seen. I nodded and watched him punch the buttons on the phone. The house across the street was dark.

'Inspector Sexton, this is Superintendent Kevin Sherrin, Eastern Division. I'm outside your home. I know you have a woman inside and I believe she's there against her will. I want you to allow her to leave.'

The answer was brief and evidently surprised him.

'Okay,' Sherrin said.

'What's he say?' I whispered.

Sherrin ignored me and spoke into the phone. 'What? Yes, he's here. Okay.'

He rang off and pocketed the phone. 'He wants

us to go in. You too. He says he doesn't intend to hurt anyone.'

'But he won't let Glen go?'

He stood. 'No. Coming?'

He watched as I unclipped the Smith & Wesson from under the dashboard. 'You do anything with that unless I tell you to and I'll fucking shoot you myself.'

I had an old bomber jacket in the back of the car. I stripped off my blazer and put the jacket on. The gun fitted easily into one of its pockets. I followed Sherrin across the street, trotting to catch up with his long strides. Lights came on in the house as we went through the gate. The path was slightly overgrown and already wet from the rain. We got wetter as we pushed past the shrubbery.

A set of concrete steps led up to a wide, deep porch with a tile roof. We stepped in out of the rain and I wiped my face on my sleeve. The old jacket smelled of sweat and dust. Sherrin barely broke stride; he jerked open the flyscreen, turned the handle on the door and walked into the house.

29

'In here.'

We tracked the voice through a dim entrance and passage to a living room where lights were shining brightly. The man sitting on the two-seater couch fitted Craig's description exactly — tallish, early middle age, fit-looking, balding, cop moustache. He held what looked like a Glock eight-millimetre pistol. Held it steadily. Glen, in her smart dress and jewellery and minus her coat, was sitting on a chair to his left. She was handcuffed to the arm of the chair by the left wrist. She held a half full glass in her right hand. There was a bottle of Johnny Walker Black Label on a low table beside Sexton.

He moved the pistol a centimetre, no more. 'Weapons on the floor or I shoot her this instant.'

His voice was vibrant and steady and he looked perfectly capable of doing what he said. Sherrin took his service pistol from an underarm holster and dropped it on the carpet. I followed suit with the .38. With his eyes fixed steadily on us, Sexton took a pair of US-style ratchet plastic restraints and tossed them to Sherrin.

'Cuff Hardy to the chair with those around both wrists and the chair arm. Then you sit down in front here.'

'You said you didn't want to hurt anyone,' Sherrin said.

The Glock moved again. 'Did I? Do it!'

I sat in an overstuffed chair about two metres away. The whole room had a fussy, over-elaborate feel as if the effort made to decorate had been struggling against the drawback of bad taste. Sherrin fastened the restraints and then sat where Sexton had directed. He was doing everything by the book in a hostage situation, except that we had no back-up.

Glen was watching all this as if it were something on a screen and she wasn't really present. She raised the glass to her mouth and took a slug.

'Glen!' Sherrin yelped.

'Shut up!' Sexton lifted his own glass and took a solid drink.

Sherrin drew in a breath and I could feel the effort it was taking him to calm down from across the room. 'How are we going to resolve this?'

'It's resolved, Super,' Sexton said. 'There's nothing left to say.' He turned his head fractionally towards Glen but the pistol didn't move. 'You ready?'

Glen finished what was in her glass and closed her eyes. 'Yes.'

Sexton shot her through the temple.

'No,' Sherrin screamed. He dived for his gun and Sexton shot him through the top of his skull where his hair was thinnest.

I didn't move a muscle. The air in the room filled with the smell of cordite and the strange, salty tang of blood. Glen's head was a pulpy mass and bone and brain matter spewed from Sherrin's wound. Blood flowed freely from the part of his head that remained and he twitched for a few seconds before becoming still. The sight fascinated me until I managed to blink and look elsewhere.

Sexton let the pistol drop as he poured himself some more Scotch. He drank and looked across at me as if I'd just arrived and had taken a seat. 'She asked me to do it,' he said. 'Begged me.'

I forced down the nausea and nodded at Sherrin. 'What about him?'

'Poor bugger,' he said. 'Obsessed by her and with no fucking chance at all. I know all about that.'

Plastic restraints have to be cut off. There's no other way. I was hoping that Sherrin hadn't fastened them properly, had given me an out. But he'd played it by the book right to the end. I could've got to my feet and gripped the chair arm and swung it . . . and been dead before I had it off the floor. How loud had the shots been? Quite loud, but in a brick house on a big block with rain falling and the TVs on all around? No chance. I was sitting in a room with an armed multiple murderer who was holding all the cards. If I was religious I'd have been saying my prayers. I wasn't. I was very afraid . . . and very curious.

'So,' I said. 'What now.'

He sighed and looked around the room. 'My life

turned to shit a while ago, Hardy. My wife left me and took the kids. Not much of a wife and pretty hopeless kids, but still . . . And the crap's hit the fan at the station. I'm for the chop. Nothing much. A few bucks here and there but you know how it is when the hunt's on. I'm gone.'

'Harkness?'

He knocked back some more Scotch. Would he drink himself blind before he could shoot me? Not likely. 'All this happens and I hear fucking Rodney St John Harkness is getting out of the loony bin.' He laughed. 'I'd been trying to find ways of getting to him for years. Then I met these dick-head civil liberties lawyers and I gave them the steer. It took a fair while but they did the job.' He laughed again, a cracked, broken bark. It gave me something else to think about.

I could see then that he was quite mad, thrown way off balance by adversity and stress mixed with booze and guilt and God knows what else. It didn't help. He was still a killer, skilled with guns and obviously with no thoughts of the future. Despite the jacket and the warm moist air, I began to feel cold.

'You killed them quickly,' I said. 'Why did you do what you did to Harkness?'

'Your lady friend here told me you've found out about Juliet and Lucille. Harkness killed Juliet as surely as if he'd driven over her, and what he did to Lucille and Rose . . . She was my daughter, not his. Lucille told me. She was going to leave him . . .'

'But why torture him?'

He didn't answer for what seemed like a full minute but probably wasn't. 'I wanted to know where he'd put them and he wouldn't tell me. So I burned him. Then he said he hadn't killed them, so I cut off his finger. Then . . .'

He was close to some kind of nervous collapse and the odds were that he'd make a clean sweep. I didn't know whether to encourage him to keep talking or try to steer him in some other direction. But I knew it was out of my hands when he laughed.

'That poor bastard. What a couple of losers. He told me . . . he told me that Lucille killed Rose and herself. She was all fucked-up with anti-depressants and booze and other stuff and she fed Rose the pills and took them herself and she died. He buried them and he went mad. I believe him. Yeah, the way he was by then, I believe him.'

'But you killed him.'

There was another long pause and I had to break it or fall to pieces myself. 'Glen just fronted up to you?'

He nodded. 'With her little gun. But she didn't care. Scarcely resisted. She wanted out and Harkness, he was the same. Begged me in the end.'

I felt he was working himself up to it and I wanted to delay it as long as possible for no good reason.

'How did you find Harkness? How did you know what to feed the lawyers?'

'I had help. A volunteer. You work it out.'

'What about the kid?'

'Kid?'

'The junkie who saw you break into the flat in Bondi.'

'Don't know what you're talking about.' He glanced at Glen and then down at Sherrin and he smiled. 'You know something? The old saying's wrong. Three's company.'

He put the Glock under his chin above the Adam's apple and pulled the trigger.

30

'D'you need counselling?' Jerry asked.

'No.' I said.

'I'm not sure. You spent over an hour in a room with three dead bodies, one of them your former lover.'

We were in her yard four days later after all the cop comings and goings, fending off the journalists, catching up on sleep. I was still dealing with the grief over Glen. Jerry was nervous.

'When I was a soldier,' I said, 'I had people shot all around me and shot some myself. No lovers, I admit, but we didn't do counselling. We just got on with it.'

'No scars?'

'Who knows? Do you see me twitching, having nightmares?'

'No,' she said. 'I guess your stoicism's intact.'

'Is that what it is, Jerry? How's yours?'

'What d'you mean?'

'You know what I mean. Sexton as good as told me. Rod came here and you held him somewhere for Sexton.'

She turned her head away to look out at the

water. Her voice seemed to be coming from a different set of vocal cords. 'He raped me in Rutherford House. Should I have let him get away with it? I knew Sexton from some time ago when I counselled him after a police shooting. I knew about him and Lucille and . . . Rodney. I knew Sexton wanted him out and I helped. Willingly. We thought he'd come to me sooner or later.'

She'd changed her tune on sex with Rod. I gathered my car keys from the table and stood up.

She looked at me. 'You've got no proof, Cliff. And the rest of it, between us, was real.'

'It's a shitty world,' I said.

I'd given the police a statement that went back to the beginning and followed all the ins and outs of the Harkness business. Almost all. It ended up so long I got writer's cramp initialling the pages. Warren Harkness came to see me after the police had interviewed him.

'You were less than generous towards my mother and myself in your statement.'

'I don't feel generous towards you.'

'Nevertheless, we are prepared to be generous to you in return for information.'

I didn't say anything. We were in my office and I hadn't invited him to sit down. He stood in front of my desk and I waited for him to go on.

'Yes, if you can tell us anything about the disposal of the bodies of . . .'

My look stopped him right there. He cleared his throat, turned and walked out. The broadsheets covered the case clinically; the tabloids had gone to town. Neither treatment made the Harknesses look good. It was a small compensation to go with one other — apparently I hadn't made Craig a target for Sexton.

I gave evidence at the inquests but I didn't go to the funerals. I decided to give up on funerals. The one I'll have to go to can wait.

LUGARNO

A Cliff Hardy Novel

Peter Corris

I was about to punch in the numbers when a man loomed up beside me. When I say loomed I mean loomed – he was tall and wide with a shaven head, and the pale hand that plucked the mobile from my grasp and threw it away was super-sized.

'Hey,' I protested.

He just stood there, a pace away now – a hundred kilos of bone and muscle in T-shirt and jeans. I had a gun and a tyre iron and I thought I'd need both to make an impression on him, but they were in the car. For now, it was just me.

When it's only twenty-four hours into a new case and PI Cliff Hardy's already been heavied, you know that the job is going to get his full attention. Cliff has been hired by high-flying consultant Martin Price to find out who's been supplying heroin to Price's teenage daughter – who in turn has got her beautiful young stepmother hooked.

The leafy, well-heeled suburb of Lugarno seems an unlikely hotbed of drug-dealing and corruption, but Cliff is finding out the hard way that crime and violence come calling even at posh waterside addresses.

07786
553799

THE OTHER SIDE OF SORROW

A Cliff Hardy Novel

Peter Corris

Corruption, murder and a missing girl: routine for Cliff Hardy – except this time it's personal.

Cliff Hardy is stunned to get a phone call from his ex-wife Cynthia. It's been more than twenty years since she last shouted she never wanted to see him again . . . and she was never a woman to change her mind. But that surprise is nothing to the bombshell Cynthia is about to drop. Dying of cancer, she's desperate to get in contact with the daughter she gave up for adoption – and the daughter in question, she confesses, is also Cliff's!

A shocked but sceptical Cliff agrees to search for their missing daughter. But this was never going to be a straightforward investigation . . .

The Other Side of Sorrow brings all of Peter Corris's consummate crime-writing skills to an intriguing, emotionally charged plot.

BANTAM PAPERBACK